wherethekissingneverstops

Books by Ron Koertge

The Arizona Kid

The Brimstone Journals

Margaux with an X

Shakespeare Bats Cleanup

Stoner & Spaz

Where the Kissing Never Stops

wherethekissingneverstops

RON KOERTGE

CANDLEWICK PRESS
CAMBRIDGE, MASSACHUSETTS

Copyright © 1986, 2005 by Ron Koertge

Second paperback edition 2005

The Library of Congress has cataloged the hardcover as follows:

Koertge, Ronald.
Where the kissing never stops / Ron Koertge. — 1st Candlewick Press ed.
p. cm.
Summary: While trying to cope with his father's death, his mother's new job as a stripper, and his own libido, high-school junior Walker meets a new girl who makes life seem pretty wonderful after all.
ISBN 0-7636-2543-4 (hardcover)
[1. Coming of age — Fiction. 2. Mothers and sons — Fiction.
3. High schools — Fiction. 4. Schools — Fiction.] I. Title.
PZ7.K81825Wh 2005
[Fic] — dc22   2004062852

ISBN 0-7636-2696-1 (paperback)

2 4 6 8 10 9 7 5 3 1

Printed in the United States of America

This book was typeset in Cushing and Tania

Candlewick Press
2067 Massachusetts Avenue
Cambridge, Massachusetts 02140

visit us at www.candlewick.com

For Bianca

Thanks also to Merrill Joan Gerber,
Mary Rocamora, and Helen Rosenstock

chapter 1

"What took you so long?" Sully asked when I finally got to the phone.

"I was busy."

"Yeah? Doing what?"

"Not that. If you must know, I was just putting away the potato chips and brownies."

"Bring some when you come over."

"Who said I was coming over?"

"Look at it this way, Walker: it's hot, my dad filled the pool, and there are three *Playboy* bunnies here, all centerfolds."

"Two for you, naturally."

"I'm the host. By the way, don't tell your mom."

"Mom's not home. She's interviewing for a job."

"Great. How long's it been now, almost a year? That's enough time to be sad. A job is just the thing."

"Thank you, Dr. Sullivan."

"Go ahead and make fun, but when I get to be a big-time psychiatrist, that kind of insight will cost you plenty."

"I thought you wanted to be a surgeon, like your dad."

"I might. I have lots of career choices."

"Lucky you. I just got my ASVAB back from counseling. Guess where my aptitudes lie."

"Is there a category for masturbation?"

"Only as a hobby, not as a profession. Try preacher or forest ranger."

"You?"

"Yeah."

"Well, could you be both?"

"Why not? 'All you bears who are sorry you ate that family from Iowa, come forward and we'll pray. And you nasty trees, stop rubbing your limbs together.' "

" 'And you squirrels, cover up your nuts.' " Sully laughed at his own joke, then said, "Hurry up. I'll meet you out there."

Sully's folks had a really nice house about ten minutes away from mine. On the way over, I stopped at an AM-PM Mini-Mart, locked my bike just to be on the safe side, bought a package of Twinkies, then sat outside in the sun to eat them. I wondered if I should be a forest ranger. Maybe I could get a job so high in the mountains there wouldn't be any junk food. I pictured myself lean and hard from living on cold water and rocks, rescuing girls in torn shorts and halter tops. Their gratitude knew no bounds.

God, I thought about sex a lot. Maybe it was the season. Maybe my young man's fancy was turning.

Sully was stretched out on a chaise when I got there. He tapped his watch and frowned.

"What took you so long?"

"I had to find my trunks."

"In that room of yours? I'm surprised you didn't get here tomorrow. You can change anywhere; there's nobody home."

I put my towel under a chair. "In a minute."

The truth was, I was afraid my stomach would hang over my waistband. There were fish on my trunks; it would look like they were swimming under a ledge.

"I had Twinkies on the way over," I said, lying down on the webbed chaise.

"It's good for you to confess, my son," Sully said. "Don't be ashamed. We're all human, except me, who is perfect." Then he propped himself up on one elbow. He was wearing dark sunglasses and I couldn't see his eyes. "You've only been pigging seriously since Debbie left, haven't you?"

"Four months is quite a stretch if you're chewing the whole time."

"You've had a hell of a year." He patted me on the shoulder: *bam-bam*. Guy-pats. Just like at the funeral. Just before my mother and I fell in the grave. God, what a mess.

"You know," I said, and I could feel my chest get thick, "for years everything was fine. Maybe I was a little overweight, maybe I jerked off a little more than was good for me, but that was it. Then my father dies, just like that." I snapped my fingers. "Then I meet Debbie. We start to go together. Maybe she's not the prettiest girl in the world."

"Or the tallest."

"Or the tallest."

"Or the smartest."

"Okay, but she was really nice to me, Sully. I mean really. And she never looked at another guy."

"And you're still a virgin."

"So are you."

"I didn't go steady with anybody."

4

"And then she moved away. It was like she'd died, too. One week she's here, the next week she's gone."

"My father says that adolescence is the most difficult period in a person's life. He says growing up is just a bitch. And let's face it, we're growing up. I go away to Harvard next year, and you'll be a senior."

I was only half listening. "What next, I wonder? I mean, my father and Debbie are two. Mom says bad things come in threes."

"You need a girlfriend."

"And so do you."

"Bullshit," he said mildly, turning over to show the sun another million freckles. "I need to get older is all. High-school girls like cute guys — lots of hair, nice bodies, the whole package. That's not me."

"You make it sound like you're some kind of troll."

"Not at all. I'm just realistic. Besides, I don't have time for a girlfriend: three years of high school, three years of college, med school, intern, and residency, and I'm out even faster than my old man was."

"Marcia Notley likes you."

"My father says I can't afford the Marcia Notleys of this world."

"What does that mean?"

"Marcia Notley wants to get married, and she wants to marry a doctor. My father says all women secretly want to marry doctors. That's why I've got to watch my step from here on out."

"Yeah, there's a beauty lurking behind every bush."

"But that doesn't mean *you* can't have a girlfriend."

"Old careerless, goalless Walker."

"Still." He sat up and put on a green plaid shirt. "It'd be nice to have some girls in my pool right now."

"We could make them promise they wouldn't want to marry you before they ever got in the water."

"Then when they jumped in, all their tops would fall off."

"I saw somebody's breast in a pool once."

"By itself?"

"Well, obviously it wasn't taking a dip on its own. I guess it'd just slipped out of this girl's suit. She was standing there down toward the deep end and I guess she didn't notice."

"Did it float?"

"Sort of, I guess."

"My dick floats."

"Gee, Sully, let me call the newspaper. There's probably time to make tomorrow's edition."

"Doesn't yours?"

"To my undying credit, I don't know. But then, you're a bachelor doctor with keener powers of observation than us forest ranger pastors."

6

"Was it pretty?"

"Her breast? Sort of; not very sexy, though. It looked friendly bobbing in the water like that."

"My father says the parts of the body are interesting, but grotesque."

"Tell that to Hugh Hefner. Anyway, Sully, your father's married and settled in. I'll bet twenty years ago he didn't take off your mom's bra and say, 'Interesting, dear, but grotesque.'"

"Have you ever touched one?"

"Bare?"

"Uh-huh."

"Almost."

"With Debbie?" he asked.

"Who else? It was nice."

"God, I'll bet."

"You never touched Peggy's?"

"Peggy's a friend. We go to concerts and stuff sometimes. Hell, Walker, Peggy's your friend, too."

"Sure, but not like you."

Suddenly he sat up and pulled his jeans half on. Not to his knees, though; I mean he only put one leg in.

"I think I'll perform a scientific experiment. I'll tan this leg until it's a golden brown."

"Like Colonel Sanders's drumsticks?"

"Maybe all the freckles will run together and I'll be

tanned forever. Then I'll show the leg to a few girls and if they like it I'll tan the rest of me."

"I'd like to be there when you tell those select few that you've got this leg you want them to evaluate."

"Quiet. My father says tissue can be affected by thought. I'm going to think this leg dark in just thirty minutes."

When I opened my eyes, it was cold. Sully was still lying there. He was breathing evenly and his mouth was half open. I guess that's what happens when you marry somebody, or at least sleep together. You see her drool and stuff like that. I'd never seen a girl drool. I knew they went to the bathroom — everybody does — but neither Sully nor I had ever heard one fart. Belch maybe, but not the other. Sully said it was the same thing. I said that it wasn't. I said that there were some countries where it was polite to belch after a meal but nowhere was it polite to fart afterward. He said I was exaggerating. We almost got into a fight over it, but that was when we were a lot more immature. Like last year.

"I'm not asleep," he said.

"Who said you were? Be like my mother and tell me you were just resting your eyes."

"God, I slobbered on myself."

"Maybe you were just resting your lips, too." I stood up and reached for my towel.

"What's the hurry? Stay and eat dinner if you want. We're having steak again."

"We're having Caviar Helper. Add it to anything and it's twice as expensive. Thanks anyway."

I started to pedal home, taking my time, making those smooth skier's swoops that cover the whole street, the same kind I'd made ever since I was a kid.

Spring had definitely arrived. There were those early bulbs my mother had put in every year but this one — the crocuses and daffodils and one or two more whose names I couldn't remember. And the grass was coming in fast, looking eager and new.

Somebody in a red Subaru honked and waved. A bike is okay, but there's nothing like a car. Man, just get in a car and everything changes; it's like a room on wheels. Nothing can happen on a bike; anything can happen in a car.

Still, you can't look around as much or ride real slow without having somebody call Neighborhood Watch. Pedaling, though, I could enjoy the trip. It was late and people were going home for dinner. Sometimes I could see through the front windows where the curtains were pulled to one side like an old-fashioned hairdo. There sat the family with the dishes going around from hand to hand. It was eerie the way that scene repeated itself that evening: family after family eating and smiling at each other, not in that gross way with spinach stuck to somebody's front tooth, but in a nice way, probably just telling stories about what happened at work or school that day.

I have to admit, it made me want to see my mother.

The Saturn was in the drive, and I went in wondering what was for dinner —"like a lamb to the slaughter," as my father used to say about some poor guy who didn't see it coming.

Inside, my mom was staring at the stove. The stereo was on real loud and she was dancing a little, swishing her behind and pushing herself off the Amana into little spins like her partner was too fat to move.

"Hey," she said when she saw me. "I got a job."

"Great. Doing what?"

"I don't want to cook. I thought maybe we'd go out and celebrate. Have a pizza or something."

"Okay, I guess."

"I'm going to have a glass of wine first. You want to sit with me while I have a glass of wine?"

Man, what a fool I was. Hadn't I had parents for six-teen years and didn't I know their tricks? Or maybe I was just thinking about the pizza I would order, the one that took two men to lift and had everything on it but beets.

"I want you to hear this from me," she said, turning down the stereo.

"Hear what?" The alarms were starting to go off, but faintly.

"That job I got? I'm going to be a dancer."

"What kind of dancer? Like you were in college?"

"Sort of."

I sat back and looked at her carefully. She took a sip of wine and her lips were as shiny as her eyes.

"Where are you going to dance?" I was getting very wary.

"At a club just outside Kansas City." She felt for the top buttons of her blouse.

"There's something going on," I said, "isn't there? Something I'm not going to like."

"It's up to you, really. You can like it or not like it. I hope you like it. I hope you're proud of me."

"You aren't going to move out or anything, are you? And leave me here?"

"Oh, honey, no. God." She put her wineglass down and reached for my hands, but I pulled them back. I felt like a little animal with his paws curled up on his chest.

"Tell me," I said.

She sighed and sat back. "I'm working at a club called Ye Olde Burlesque. I'm one of the exotic dancers."

"You?"

"Your old bag of a mother, you mean?"

"Why?"

"I needed a job."

"A job? Sarah Willoughby's mother works at Sears. Kevin Kopit's mother works at OSH. They didn't get jobs taking off their clothes."

"That's their business."

"Ye Olde Burlesque sounds stupid. It's such a stupid name. It's Middle English and nineteenth century all mixed together. There wasn't any burlesque in the Middle Ages. There was just Ye Olde Black Death and Ye Olde Inquisition."

"It's old-fashioned burlesque," she said patiently. "That's all. It's to show that there's comedy sketches and singers as well as dancers."

"Topless dancers?"

"Exotic dancers. It's not a dirty show."

"I suppose you put on more clothes and pray."

"I do what's called a novelty act."

"Oh, God. Don't tell me." I actually began to wring my hands. I'd heard of that all my life, and there I was, doing it. "You didn't even ask me."

"It's none of your business."

"Are you crazy? I have to take the fallout. Everybody's going to know. All the kids at school. What am I supposed to say?"

"Tell them the truth."

"That you show your ass to anybody?"

"Watch your mouth with me, Walker. I'm still your mother."

"Then act like it." I was starting to shout.

"Look. I took the job. I told them I'd be there. I won't go back on my word."

"When do you start? Maybe I can move to another town and grow a beard."

"Tonight. The snake got sick, and Eve can't do very much without a snake."

"I don't believe I'm hearing this."

"Sweetheart," she said, leaning toward me, "I thought about this before I did it, and I know I want this job." A fingernail tapped each word into the coffee table. "Anyway, who's going to know? I'm not going to tell, if that's what you're worried about."

"They'll see you. Everybody will see you. Probably somebody we know will be there tonight, and tomorrow it'll be all over school."

"Walker, be reasonable. Who'll drive forty miles one way to see old-fashioned burlesque in a club that doesn't hold two hundred people?"

"You, that's who. You'll drive it every night."

"Sure, but I have to."

"Why? Is this some kind of a midlife crisis?"

"Honey, we need the money."

The stupid rhyme just irritated me. "I wish Dad was alive. He wouldn't let you do this."

"Isn't that the truth," she said, smiling the tiniest smile. Then she sat back on the couch and finished her wine, closing both eyes and letting the liquid trickle down her throat. God, what would she do next, start smoking cigarettes and wearing a red dress?

She stood up decisively and held out one hand. "C'mon, let's go and get a giant pepperoni."

"I don't eat pizza." The Glacier speaks.

"With exotic dancers?"

"Period."

"Oh, pooh. Your room smells like Shakey's about half the time."

That made me blush. I thought I'd been so clever. "Okay then. I don't want to eat with you. How's that?"

"Honest." She leaned over and shook her hair, which was dark and curly and shiny. "Dumb but honest."

"I think I'll go to my room." I sounded like I was punishing myself.

"Suit yourself, but first give a listen. I have to work

six nights a week," she said evenly, "but never any later than ten-thirty or eleven. I don't leave until six, so I won't be gone very long. There's a list of phone numbers on the pad, and the neighbors know I'll be away."

"Oh, Jesus. What'd you say you'd be doing?"

"Well, I thought of telling them the truth and saying that I was making two hundred dollars a night as an actress and a dancer in a revival of old-time burlesque, but I knew they'd sew a scarlet *A* on my best sweater and dunk me in the river, so I said I was drowning kittens for a dollar an hour and that seemed to satisfy them."

"Don't just do it for the money," I begged. "I'll go to work. I'll stop eating so much."

"You won't go to work," she said firmly. "You'll keep studying, you'll get terrific grades, and you'll get a scholarship to college."

"I can work and still get A's, honest."

"Out of the question."

"You sound like Dad. That's what he said when you wanted to go to work two years ago."

"I got a part-time job in a pet store, that's all, and he acted like . . ." She leaned toward me. "Walker, it's not just the money. I think I'm going to like it."

"Stripping?"

"Dancing." She corrected me like a teacher.

"Well, I hate it."

She sighed. "I still need to eat dinner. You can come with me and I'll drop you back here, or I'll go alone and just drive straight to Love's Park from Luigi's."

So that's where it was. How ironic. Love's Park was Kansas City's sleaziest suburb. Sully and I had been over there to see some films. They were always shown at art theaters and they were usually about some naive girl who moved to the big city and had about sixteen affairs before lunch. Girls named Monique.

"Give me a kiss, okay?" Mom was standing there with both arms open. At her feet were a purse and an overnight bag. She might have been leaving on a short trip. Or forever.

I shook my head and stepped back. Just before she turned away, I saw her lips bunch up and I knew I'd hurt her. A little part of me was glad, but all the rest felt terrible.

When the back door closed, I crept out to the kitchen, peeked through the blinds, and followed the red taillights through the chilly evening until they disappeared around the corner.

Then I wandered around the house for a while. God, it felt big. Isn't it funny how just one other person can fill a place up?

My mom had had a lot of Dad's stuff taken out of the house and stored, and I can't say that I blame her. He had this one stupid bowling trophy he was very proud of, and she just couldn't look at it sitting up there on the mantel without going all to pieces. I don't know where he got the trophy; I never saw him in a shirt with his name on the pocket. Maybe he bowled in a suit. He did most everything else in one. Even when we played catch on the lawn, he was dressed for a board meeting. Maybe that's why my mom wanted to take all her clothes off. She'd never done it before.

I began to wonder about my dad. It was starting to look like there'd been things going on that I didn't know about, not that that's a big surprise. Kids don't think about their folks nearly as much as everybody imagines. Parents are just there, like background music at the mall. In fact, that's a lot of what I missed about my dad — his thereness. All I really had left was Mom and this Dad-shaped space.

I was about as hungry as I was upset, but then hardly anything ever got in the way of my appetite. If a giant meteor hits and I survive, I'll probably be the only one looting a deli.

It was pretty bad setting the table for nobody but myself. I remembered how right after the funeral Mom would forget while she was dealing out plates and automatically put one down for Dad, too. Then she'd cry again, sometimes right into the casserole.

I had to wait until nine to call Sully. His parents all but locked him in his room right after dinner so he'd study. They'd take a message, but I sure didn't want to leave information like this lying around on pink phone pads. Mrs. Sullivan didn't have much to do except gossip. She made the town crier look like the patron saint of silence.

"You're kidding," said Sully.

"Is that why I'm laughing so much?"

"Medically, this is very interesting."

"If I get you a couple of cadavers and a thunderstorm, can you make me a new mother?"

"It's good you still have a sense of humor, unless these jokes are just symptoms of a complete breakdown."

"Love your bedside manner."

I could almost hear him lean forward. "What did I tell you, Walker? She came up out of that grave looking like a new woman. Hold it."

"What?" I looked around my living room.

"Hang on until I can find some privacy. My folks have to watch *60 Minutes.*"

I didn't want to, but I started thinking about the

funeral. My father said in his will that he wanted everybody to watch him go and wave bye-bye. Those were his exact words. See, my mom used to stand on the porch every morning and do just that. Rain or shine there she'd be, with her arms folded like women do, and then when he'd backed out and hit Monterey Road, she'd wave.

So there we were at the cemetery. Everybody was crying or trying not to, the six guys were letting him down with those green canvas tapes, and we were leaning over, waving bye-bye, when my aunt Avanelle, who was standing behind me, passed out. We were packed in there, and it was the domino effect pure and simple. I went first and then Mom.

The next thing I remember is that I could see up everybody's dress. It was gross, but it was also pretty exciting in a weird way. I mean everything had been so black — black dresses and shoes, black stockings and suits. All of a sudden there were those colored underpants: pink and white and even red. Besides getting me a little turned on, it helped me get my bearings. Everything wasn't all grief.

Naturally, they hauled us out and brushed the dirt off, nobody was hurt, and it didn't turn into a fad, thank God, like people at a party jumping into the pool with their clothes on.

But Sully did say a little later that my mom came out of that hole a different person. He said he could see it in her eyes.

"Did she say why?" he asked once he'd settled in his own room.

"She just needs a job."

"That's not all of it."

"You're telling me. And speaking of telling, promise me you won't tell anybody."

"Don't worry. Listen, what do you think she's trying to prove?"

"I don't know. That she can drive me nuts?"

"It's not about you, I'll bet. It's about her saying, 'Hey, look at me. I'm still alive and I'm still pretty.' She is pretty, too. She always kind of reminds me of Elizabeth Taylor in *National Velvet* — you know, with those curls and that white skin."

"I'll trade my mom and my CD collection for your mom."

"Look. Maybe it won't last long. What do we know? Maybe tonight's the only night. Maybe it won't be what she expects at all. Maybe it'll be embarrassing. Maybe it's just a fling, a one-time thing."

"Do you think so?"

"No. It's not good to get your hopes up and then have them dashed."

"Get them up. They've already been dashed." Then I took a quick, deep breath. "Oh, God. I just thought of something. You know how I said bad things come in threes? This is the third thing. My dad, Debbie, and now this."

"Now you sound like your father. Remember how superstitious he was?"

"Sully, do you think my dad was the dad I knew?"

"Run that by me again?"

"Do you think that all there was to my father was what I could see?"

"You mean was he more than a supervisor at the phone company and your dad?"

"Yeah, I guess."

"Sure, there was more."

"Then who was I crying about when he died? Who do I still miss, today more than ever?"

"Ask your mom."

"Are you kidding? Why would she tell me anything?"

"She had to have said something already, or you wouldn't be thinking like this."

He had me there. "Isn't that the truth," she'd said when I'd pointed out that Dad wouldn't have let her be a stripper.

"Anyway," Sully said, "I've got just what you need to take your mind off your troubles."

"Thirty pounds of chocolate decadence?"

"A girl."

"I don't need a girl."

"You do. Now more than ever."

"And what would I tell her my mother does for a living?"

"Lie."

"That's a wonderful way to start a relationship."

"Her name is Rachel Gardner. She just transferred from California or New York, I forget which. She's in two of my accelerated classes."

"Is she pretty?"

"Sort of. She's got an okay face with short hair and —"

"I don't want to go out with a girl who has short hair on her okay face."

"I think she's got a good body, but it's hard to tell with all those clothes. I did get a glimpse of one leg the other day in physics and it looked fine."

"So far she has a beard and one good leg."

"She's at least as good-looking as Debbie, and she's rich."

"So what would she want with me?"

"Just to go out. She's lonely. She doesn't know anybody in town. You need this girl. She needs you. Two lonely souls. She hasn't got a mother."

"Shouldn't we call the Pope? Isn't that a miracle?"

"She died. Listen, meet me after math tomorrow. I'll introduce you."

"No."

"Look in the paper. Find something to tempt her — a movie, a concert, anything."

"She'll be busy."

"When you talk to her, don't be put off by any aloofness, okay? It'll just be a defense. You can bust through that icy facade."

"I'll just throw my body against it."

"You aren't fat."

"No? Then why do the Pillsbury Doughboy and I wear the same size shorts?"

I really was hysterical. That wasn't always my style. Or it didn't used to be. Had I changed? Had I emerged from that box-shaped hole a different person, too?

Sully had to get back to his books; Sully always had to get back to his books. I tried studying, but my mind wouldn't stay put. I kept picturing my mom onstage, in the spotlight, while lowlifes waved dollar bills and left their fingerprints all over her shoes.

Who needed to study, anyway? Anybody who couldn't graduate from high school with about one hour of concentrated studying a week was better off being a forest ranger. I admit, I wasn't taking those high-tech accelerated classes, but what was the big hurry? I just wasn't like Sully with his career map: all those straight lines from high school to college to medical school. My map would have been like the ones you see in museums, full of blank spaces and sea monsters and landmasses with no name.

In spite of myself I scanned the entertainment pages. What would a girl from California like to do? There was very little surfing in Missouri.

Back to the books. God, I hated *Silas Marner.*

TV time. *NYPD Blue* cops in a rowdy bar full of drug addicts and felons. They were looking for a topless dancer who'd been kidnapped.

So I tried the more obscure channels — land of the nonstop evangelist, Korean variety hour and, on the educational network, the usual close-up of a lizard. I settled for *The Farm Report,* a slow crawl of prices for soybeans, hog bellies, and wheat.

But it soothed me. The next thing I knew, something woke me up. Some sound. Tentacles? Pods cracking open? The rustle of a silk-lined cape?

It's funny, but whenever Mom was home and I heard something, I got my baseball bat and went to take a look. This time I scurried into my bedroom and locked the door. Protecting somebody else is easy; taking care of yourself is a whole other thing.

Pretty soon I heard her car, and I have to admit I was relieved. I unlocked the bedroom door and pretended to be asleep. Man, people are weird. Look at me — open the door so she can peek in, and then act like it doesn't matter.

Maybe I wanted it both ways. I wanted to make sure she still loved me, but I didn't want to see her in some embarrassing outfit. What if she wore her work clothes home, tassels and all? Who would see her, and who would they tell? Would everybody at school know by first period?

What I wanted was to go down to breakfast next morning and find her standing at the stove, wearing two or three aprons, cooking up stacks of pancakes, and apologizing all over the place.

Instead we got to the kitchen at just about the same time. I could see a sequin or some sparkly stuff right near the corner of one eye. Man, it looked out of place, especially since she was wearing the robe Dad had given her for Christmas last year.

She nodded at me coolly.

"So, how was it?" I asked.

Disgusting. Stupid. A real mistake. Only a passing fancy. I must have been out of my mind. Harmless but silly. I wouldn't go back there for a million dollars. Once was enough, believe me.

"Fine." She moved her shoulders under the salmon-colored chenille and shook her dark curly hair. "Hard, though. It'll take me a while to get in shape."

"So you're going back?"

She looked at me evenly. "Sure." It was a little like a cowboy movie. She might have said "Yup," or "It's your move, stranger." And God knows I felt like one.

"I'm hungry. What sounds good, Walker?"

"You don't have to fix anything for me. You're so tired. I ate dinner alone; I can eat breakfast alone."

She let it slide by. The Teflon effect on sarcasm. "You should eat; you know all those studies about a good breakfast and success in the classroom."

"I'll get some doughnuts."

"It's your body; you're grown-up enough to pollute it if you want to."

"How much money do we have?"

"Enough."

"How much is that? If I'm so grown-up, why don't I know?"

Deliberately she broke two eggs into a skillet, then she held up two more. "Are you sure you don't . . ."

"Quit treating me like a kid — I mean it."

"Stop acting like one, then."

I could feel the tears, but they were a long way off, down at my knees or maybe even in my shoes. I hadn't cried since the funeral.

"I hate that job of yours."

"Good. You get to hate it and I get to do it."

I sat down at the table, then got up. "But I don't want you to do it."

"I know, and I respect that. You get to feel that way and I get to dance."

"What, is dancing your whole stupid life or something?"

"I know this is hard on you," she said softly.

"Then why do it?" My heart was really going.

"Honey, I liked it. I liked dancing again."

"You liked taking off your clothes?"

"Some of the people in the audience — and if you want the truth, some of the ones I work with — would've made your dad pass out; but some of them are really nice. And anyway, even if they'd all been drooling in their beer and counting on their toes to get to eleven, I'd still like it." She smiled kind of crooked and goofy. "Maybe there's something wrong with me. Your father used to say that when he got mad. Maybe he was right."

"Why would he have passed out?"

"Walker, you know your dad. He went to church every Sunday."

"I went with him."

"Unless I'd lie for you and say I needed you around the house. And then you'd go off with Sully, and I'd lie again when he came home and say you'd just left."

"Did you lie to him about other stuff?"

27

"Sometimes."

"Do you lie to me?"

"Just so you won't worry."

"Tell me how much money we have," I demanded. "Tell me the truth."

She stared at her eggs, which, sunny-side up, were sort of staring back. Then she sighed heavily and tipped them into the garbage.

She began softly. "If your dad had lived a few more years, I'm pretty sure everything would have turned out all right."

"Don't you know?" I sounded like the relentless interrogator in a World War II movie.

"We had an arrangement. I took care of you and the house; he took care of everything else." I could see the barest smile. "Like the future."

"But he didn't, did he? Not really."

"It wasn't his fault. He didn't plan to get hit by a car in his new jogging suit. But things turned out to be in pretty much of a mess. What it boils down to is this: one insurance policy worth almost a hundred thousand dollars."

"That's a lot."

"It just sounds like a lot, honey. There could be a little more — some lawyer's still pawing through things — but I wouldn't count on it."

"And that's it?"

"We're living off the insurance money now. By the time you get ready for college, there won't be nearly enough for all four years."

"And that's why you're doing what you're doing, to send me to college?"

"Partly. And to put food on the table."

"I'll never eat anything you buy with that money."

She gave a little snort of disbelief, then pointed to the cluttered sink. "If you're never going to eat that tainted food again, why didn't you at least wash your dishes from last night?"

"You know how you just love to dance? How you can't explain it but you just love it? Well, I just love to leave dirty dishes. 'Maybe there's something wrong with me,'" I mimicked. "'But I just plain love it.'"

"You really can be a little shit, Walker. You should be ashamed of yourself."

"You should talk. You should talk about being ashamed."

That morning I peeked out the front door, wondering, I guess, if the police might not be there with a big-hearted social worker or two ready to whisk me off to the warmth and safety of some foster home where my new mother would make desserts all day and feed them to me with a golden spoon.

The street was deserted. No clucking, sympathetic neighbors, no jeering kids. Business as usual.

At school, too. No banners saying WALKER'S MOTHER IS A STRIPPER. No gutty saxophone music as I walked in, no whistles or catcalls. Nobody knew. At least not yet.

"Walker, over here."

The girl beside Sully wore a soft brown skirt, tall boots, a white swashbuckler's blouse, three or four yards of Brazilian peasant shawl, and a little mustache of perspiration. Her hair was cut jagged and pointy across the brow, and her brown eyes were big and kind of sad.

Why hadn't I dressed up a little? Why had I picked a T-shirt, much less a T-shirt with the word *T-shirt* on it? Probably she would think I was such a retard I had to have all my clothes labeled.

Sully introduced us. Her hand was warm and damp.

"You look hot," I said.

They both just stared at me. God, I could have torn out my tongue and stomped on it.

"In the weather sense, I mean. You're just wearing all those clothes and your lips are sweating."

Her pink tongue slid out to investigate. "My lips are sweating?" She seemed genuinely concerned, and her eyes got even bigger.

"Your mustache. I mean, where it would be. If you

30

had one." Ah, the life of a gravedigger. Every time I opened my mouth, I got in deeper.

"You'll have to be patient with Walker," Sully said. "He's just barely recovered from a tragic love affair."

"Sully, for God's sake."

Rachel's eyes darted from him to me, then back again, like a contestant on *Pick the Loony.*

"When Walker wouldn't be her one-and-only forever, she committed suicide."

"I had this girlfriend," I said patiently. "Her father got a job in another town and she moved."

"That's bad enough," Rachel said sympathetically. "I know what it's like to move a lot."

Then we all just stood there, moving our feet a little like the world's shyest dancers.

Finally Rachel leaned toward me. "You were going to say? . . ."

"Oh, yeah. There's this reggae concert in Kansas City this weekend, Burning Spear and —"

"God," she squealed. "I love reggae!"

Sully and I both jumped.

"Walker has his own car," said Sully.

"No, I don't."

"So it's in the shop. We'll take his mother's Cadillac." He leaned toward her. "So is it a date?" Then he leered at me and winked. "Is it a date?"

"What is this?" I whispered. "*Fiddler on the Roof*? I don't need a matchmaker. I can make my own dates."

"So do it," he hissed.

I turned to Rachel. "Uh, is it a date?"

"Sure," she said, beginning to frown and searching in both pockets like a girl mad for loose change. Sully glanced at me and shrugged. Finally, out came a card — GARDNER ENTERPRISES — with a phone number and address. "So call me, okay?"

I said that I would.

"For sure?"

"Guaranteed."

She backed away, waving all the time, so Sully and I waved, too. Then Rachel bounced off another student, turned, grabbed for her books, and was lost in the crowd. Still, I heard her from what seemed like a long way off, "Goodbye, Walter. Goodbye." It was plaintive and made the occasion seem somehow momentous. I felt like I was leaving for the war.

"You're going to make out like a bandit, Walter," said Sully, clapping his hands joyfully. "You could do anything. She doesn't even know your real name."

"I think we should definitely plan to throw her out of the car once I've taken her jewelry."

"It's not her jewelry you should be interested in."

"That reminds me. Why did you tell her all that bull-shit about my tragic love affair?"

"So she'll think you're sensitive and have deep feelings."

"And I don't have a Cadillac."

"We'll take my dad's and say it's yours."

"She'll find out."

"So? You'll probably never go out with her again, anyway."

"Why not?"

"She's got an overbite."

"Oh, well. Let's just put her out on the mountainside to die."

"I could never marry a girl who wasn't perfect."

"Who's going to marry her? We're going to a concert."

"Plus she doesn't have any breasts. And she's a little thick through the hips."

"How could you tell? She had on more clothes than —"

"Doctors know these things."

"Well, I like her. She didn't make me feel like a jerk, even though I sounded like one."

Just then, some kid went by wearing headphones.

"God," I said, "what if there's dancing?"

"What did I miss?" Sully asked, looking around.

"At the concert. What if everybody's dancing? I don't know how to dance to that kind of music. I'll probably just stand there and quiver; she'll think I'm some kind of religious fanatic."

"We'll practice. I'll bring a CD over to your place tonight."

"Since when do guys teach other guys to dance?"

"This is an emergency."

"We don't have to touch each other, do we?"

"We'll wear gloves."

I didn't want to face my mother, so I went to the library, looked at the girls for a while, studied a little — very little — then rode home slowly.

Mom didn't see me, but I spotted her turning the corner at Arlington and heading for the freeway. She sure didn't look any different; she might have been on her way to deliver guide dogs to the blind. But she wasn't.

I had barely gotten inside and put my stuff away when Sully knocked on the front door.

"I called Peggy," he said. "Everything's set for Friday."

"How's Peggy?"

He shrugged. "The same, I guess. Actually she sounded good, anxious to hear some reggae."

"She likes you; she always has."

"Get serious," he said, punching on the stereo. But before he could take his Jimmy Cliff CD out of its jewel case, on came some sleazy drum track: *boom boom bah boom.*

He looked at me quizzically. "Your mother's homework?"

"God, turn that thing off."

When Sully's music came on, I tried to get into it, but I didn't know what to do with my hands.

"Let 'em float," he said, showing me.

Sully was very good — light and supple, completely effortless.

"How's this?" I asked.

"I think you should move your feet a little; it looks like you're about to do a standing broad jump."

"Any better?" I said.

"You've got to move your arms, too. Now you're just shuffling around the floor like a janitor."

"Do you think girls really care if a guy can dance or not?"

"They seem to; at least some do."

"Do you think Rachel does?"

"Who knows?"

I seemed to be able to move my feet or my arms, but not both at the same time, like poor old Frankenstein. When I got the hands and arms right, I just stood rooted to the floor like a tree in the wind. Once I started to move my feet, though, I froze from the waist up.

"What happened?" asked Sully. "Really. You and Debbie used to dance."

"Rachel seems a lot different from Debbie."

"Rachel talks. Debbie had a smaller vocabulary than Mr. Amoeba in the Science Series."

"She talked about getting married."

"You said if you ever did, I'd be your best man. Then she up and moved on us."

"In her first letter she said she loved me and would write every day."

"Which was also the last letter, as I remember."

"Tell me about it."

"That love stuff is hard to figure. My dad says love is just a glandular misapprehension."

"Your dad should stick to surgery."

Sully kicked at the green carpet. The music throbbed in the background. Jimmy Cliff sang about love, how he'd lost it or found it or bought it or sold it or wanted it.

Love is funny stuff. Sully loved his father, but he was also scared of him, too scared to do anything but walk right where he walked, like the whole world was a mine-field. Mom said she loved me, but worked in a strip joint anyway. And Debbie, who said it a hundred times a day, wrote that one lousy letter.

* * *

For the next few days I stuck to my schedule: going to the library after school, waiting until I was sure the house was deserted, then eating dinner alone, washing my two dishes, studying, or watching TV until it was time to hide in my bedroom.

The night of the concert, though, I had to be home, and my mom came into my room holding a long envelope. She was dressed in jeans and a new Western shirt with pearl buttons and fringe across the front.

"Howdy, pardner," she said, obviously inspired by her getup. "I came to warn you about desperadoes and claim jumpers."

"What's that supposed to mean?" I said, watching her in the mirror where I was inspecting blemishes.

"Forty acres of land just outside of town." She thrust a long envelope at me. "There's a map in here and some lawyer's mumbo-jumbo, but what it boils down to is your dad left you a college education." She was smiling, obviously elated.

I took the slender white parcel. "So what do I do, sell it?"

"That's the general idea." She surveyed me. "You look nice, by the way."

"What's it worth?"

"That was a compliment; compliments are free."

"You know what I mean."

She shrugged. "I've heard everything from seventeen to seventy thousand, so it's somewhere in between. I just know that if we're careful, it'll take you through all four years."

I turned the envelope over. "And it's all mine?"

"You need my signature," she said, "in case you're thinking about buying a Corvette."

When I didn't smile back, she said, "Still mad, huh?" And when I wouldn't answer but just stared down at my shoes, polished three times, she added, "Well, you just keep making your face bleed. I'll call you when Sully comes."

"Your mom looks great," said Peggy, who sat between Sully and me in the front seat. "She asked me if I could do her hair. She said she's got this new job and wants to look good. What's the new job, anyway?"

"She works in a hospital," I said as Sully blurted out, "Bartender."

"Bartender in a hospital, huh? Does that make it okay to nurse your drinks?" She waited for somebody to laugh. "I can keep a secret, you know. If you really don't want me to say anything, I won't. I'd do anything for you guys, you know that."

"Hairdressers' gossip," I said.

"Who would I tell, anyway? The people who come

into the barber college live in rented rooms and read the *Weekly World News*. All we talk about is the alien's baby, the guy with the hiccups for twenty years, and was that a picture of Jesus on the Holy Volvo or not."

"You'll tell."

"I won't."

"She won't," said Sully.

"She's a hooker," said Peggy.

"Who is?"

"Your mom. That's the secret."

"Get serious."

"Does she have cancer? Everybody in the *Enquirer* has cancer. Elizabeth Taylor's bird had it."

"Why would my mom want to have her hair done if she had cancer?"

"What, then?"

Mumble mumble.

"I can't hear you."

"She's a stripper."

"So?"

"That's it. Isn't that enough?"

"My mom was a topless dancer for a while in the sixties. My roommate just before this one worked in the strip joints in Rantoul, Illinois. I know about five guys who want me to try it."

"You're too skinny," Sully said.

"I've got great legs. Anyway, what's the problem, Walker?"

"Just don't tell Rachel, okay?"

"What, is her father a priest or something?"

Sully — who had been creeping along a wide, curved street — pulled over to the curb.

"Just say you won't."

Peggy took my hand — clammy with nerves — and said sincerely, "You know I'd never do anything you don't want me to. You know that."

The door to Rachel's apartment was half open, and when I knocked, her father looked up from his phone conversation and motioned for me to come in. It was the same gesture I'll bet he'd used on a thousand waiters.

Their place was nice, with burgundy carpets, rose walls, and tall windows, but it looked like they had just moved in: Bekins cartons, open suitcases, a trunk, containers of cold takeout food.

"Business," he said, hanging up the phone and striding toward me. He was very outdoorsy — Wellingtons, twill pants, a shooting jacket with patches on the elbows. He even smelled like the outdoors — probably some cologne named Big Wind.

He didn't waste time with small talk, either.

"What does your father do?"

"He passed away last year."

"I'm sorry." He indicated the enormous photographs of his wife, half-hidden by fresh flowers. "I know what it's like to lose someone. How about your mother?"

"No, she's alive. I just talked to —"

"I guess I meant what does she do."

"Do?"

"Yes, your mother." He leaned forward, smiling encouragingly, like I was a quiz show contestant. "Her job," he urged.

"Oh, well." I looked around wildly. Behind him a TV murmured. Giddy housewives square-danced with enormous cans of toilet bowl cleaner.

"She dances," I began, but that was too close to the truth. Suddenly the screen filled with someone lovingly polishing her antiques. "On tables," I blurted.

He repeated slowly: "She dances on tables."

"Waits," I cried. "Waits on them. In a dance hall. Place. A dance place. A nice one. Restaurant." I was just shouting out words and phrases. It was worse than charades.

"Oh, she's a waitress!" He seemed relieved to have solved the puzzle.

"Yes, sir." No one was more relieved than I was.

"What about you, Walter?"

"Walker."

Patiently he repeated the question. "What do you want to do with your life? Later on, I mean." He looked right at me and grinned, but only half his mouth moved. "After the concert."

"I haven't really decided, sir."

"Well, you're a big, good-looking boy. You could do anything."

Except tell the truth about you-know-what.

"Ever think about land?" he continued. "There's a ton of money in land. Buying it, selling it, developing it, trading it." As he talked, he rubbed his hands together in a greedy, yum-yum motion.

"You know," I said, "it's kind of a coincidence, but I do own some land. About forty acres out there somewhere."

"Good for you. I'll buy it."

"You don't even know where it is."

"Where is it?"

"I don't know exactly."

"I'll still buy it." I half expected him to take out his checkbook and a roll of bills big as a carpet remnant.

"I think I'd like to use the bathroom." Anything to change the subject.

"Ah," he said, looking over my shoulder and opening his arms like a ringmaster. "Here she is now."

"God, Daddy," Rachel said, flustered but pleased.

"Isn't she gorgeous, Walter?"

42

"Yes, sir." A cardigan (too big) hung open to reveal a thick V-neck (also too big). Beneath that was a hint of something else. She certainly had the layered look down pat.

"Poor old Dad eats dinner alone tonight, I guess," Mr. Gardner said, hanging his head and making a big droopy-pooch pout.

"You'll be fine. Just push the button on the microwave; I marked it with a little happy-face." She brushed at his spotless jacket. "Promise me you'll chew; you know what the doctor said. And don't talk on the phone until you're done."

He nodded, turning to me. "She's a stern taskmaster," he said happily.

"There's a little surprise in the freezer for your dessert. And then some messages; I put them on your desk."

Suddenly he was all business again. "Who from? Kramer, I hope."

She shook her index finger at him. "Eat first. Look at your food like I showed you; it's your friend. Then Rice Dream. Then messages. Promise?"

"I love Rice Dream," he said, and I wondered if he was going to clap his hands.

"But after, okay?"

He nodded sheepishly. "And you two don't be late."

43

Suddenly he was all dad again: the ogre at the door. No worse than most fathers, but quite a change from the kid who couldn't wait for dessert.

"Nice outfit," said Peggy with so much enthusiasm that Rachel, settling into the back seat, looked at me doubtfully.

"Want to smoke?" Sully asked, leaning toward us with a joint.

I wasn't interested in drugs at all, only food. Still, every now and then I'd hear about somebody who got *so* high or drank *so* many beers, and I'd sort of wish I had a more dramatic vice. Nobody would ever say, "Wow, that Walker. He ate *so* many fries and *so* much cake."

Still, I didn't want Rachel to think I was a prude, so I held the smelly little thing to my lips and made a puckery face. Rachel did the same, grimacing like it was a real roach, legs still waving.

Then she leaned back and arranged her clothes. Then she smiled. I smiled back. She smiled. I smiled back. We were like ships at sea, sending silent messages with our teeth.

Finally I broke the silence. "Your dad seemed nice."

"He is. He sure acts like a big baby sometimes, though."

"You mean about . . ."

"Eating alone, yeah. Ever since Mom died, he needs all this extra attention."

She wasn't complaining, though. Not really. I could tell she liked it.

"He wants his shirts done a special way and he hates to eat alone, and he likes for me to screen his calls and go see clients with him and all kinds of stuff."

Rachel ran out of breath making her list. She sat back in the seat like just talking about her duties was exhausting. Her hand had fallen right beside mine, which was paralyzed.

I thought about giving her a consoling pat, but I didn't want her to think I was starting to grope her during the first fifteen minutes of our date.

"Why doesn't your dad just get a secretary to do all that stuff?" Peggy asked.

"He says he's too busy to find one. See, he wants to build this enormous mall and call it the Garden of Gardner." She pointed out the window. "Right around here somewhere."

"Bradleyville already has a mall over on the other side of town."

"But this isn't just a mall, you guys." She scooted forward. About a hundred yards of material piled up in her lap, but for a second I could see one smooth knee.

"This is his dream. Bigger than anything anybody ever imagined."

"Right here?" We were barely on the outskirts of town. Not ten yards away grew corn, soybeans, and spring wheat. I could smell the rich earth.

"I think so. He needs a ton of land. It's all going to be perfect, see, and completely self-sustaining. A person could be born there and grow up there and die there. He'd never have to leave the Garden."

"Wow," said Peggy, who had turned around to hear Rachel's speech.

"That's horrible," I said.

"Really? Why?"

"I don't know," I sputtered. "It just sounds horrible. To never go outside."

"Oh, you could go outside. You'd just be protected."

"I mean really outside." I rolled down the window and pointed. A huge car passed us on the left, going fifty-six to Sully's law-abiding fifty-five.

"Of course you could if you wanted to. You could get in your car and everything. But you wouldn't have to, see? Everything you'd ever want would be there." She leaned back dreamily. "Everything."

"How could you be born in a mall?" Sully said into the rearview mirror.

"In the hospital; some malls already have them. Dad

wanted my mom to have me in the Houston Galleria, but she wouldn't. Anyway, hospitals aren't any big deal. West Edmonton up in Canada has a roller coaster."

"And if you fall off, you get buried by Stiffs R Us, and then after the funeral everybody can shop."

"Gee, Walter, don't get mad. I —"

"It's Walker, not Walter. Okay?"

"Oh, God, sorry." She patted my hand, which twitched like a frog in biology lab. "You call me Raquel for a while, all right? Till we're even."

"What don't you like about malls, Walker?" she asked a few uneasy miles later.

"Yeah," boomed Peggy from the front seat. "What are you, un-American?"

"I just don't like Westgate, that's all. My dad and I went out there a couple of times and it was too weird."

"It's an old mall," Rachel said analytically, "but it's got some nice touches."

"They were playing 'Light My Fire' on the Muzak, okay?"

"Jim Morrison," moaned Peggy. "What a doll."

"And I could hardly tell what it was. Elves could have been playing it. And then 'Hey Jude,' and I could barely figure that out either."

"You aren't supposed to listen," Rachel pointed out.

47

"Music only calms you down so you can buy, or peps you up so you can buy."

"But that's just it, Raquel," I said sarcastically. "That's what I don't like about it."

"That's how you sell things, though. You make people feel safe, you get them warm or keep them cool, you get them in a good mood, and then they buy."

"Whatever happened to going downtown, where nobody hummed you to death, and just buying what you need?" I was getting steamed. "That's another thing I don't like about Westgate. Whatever happened to downtown? It's dead, that's what. Everybody's out at the mall being brainwashed."

"People are afraid of downtowns," she said. "That's why they like the malls. They're safe, Walker. Nobody ever got mugged in a mall."

"Nobody ever got mugged in downtown Bradleyville, either."

"What about Elizabeth Bartlett's father?" asked Sully.

"The guys who did that had to be from Kansas City."

"And Maureen Owens?"

"Well, she shouldn't have been down there at that time of night."

"What happened to Maureen Owens?" Rachel asked. "Was she mugged?"

"Worse," said Peggy.

"Killed?"

"Worse," said Peggy.

"Well, I don't care. I still don't like malls."

God, I sounded like some little kid talking about spinach.

When we got to the concert, the girls went to the bathroom while Sully and I hung out by the refreshment stand hoping that one of the employees would call us over and force us to buy some beer.

"It got pretty quiet in the back seat there," Sully said, "right after that impassioned plea for a bustling downtown." He looked at me quizzically. "I never knew you had such strong feelings about stuff like that."

"Did I sound dumb?"

"Just lighten up. You could do worse than marrying a land baron's daughter."

"With an overbite and no breasts?"

"How do you know that?"

"You looked at her teeth and said so."

"No, the other. Did you check?"

"Of course. I started feeling around while we were arguing. Girls always go for that."

"Just be nice, okay? She likes you."

"Do you really think so?" I wasn't being sarcastic anymore; I wanted it to be true.

I could hear a band warming up, so I practiced a few dance steps. Their muddled discord was perfect for my personal style. I'd be in trouble when they started playing together.

Peggy came up behind us, slipping both arms around Sully's waist. Rachel had her hands behind her back like she was about to recite a short poem.

"Hi," I said.

"Hi," she said back, smiling. "Are you still mad?"

I shook my head and leaned toward the wide aisle. "Let's go in."

We made our way through the crowd, losing Sully and Peggy in the process.

"Do you look different?" I asked. "Or are my senses deranged from smelling all the marijuana in the air."

"Oh, that. Peggy sort of redid my outfit."

"In the bathroom?"

"She's really neat. She just whipped out these scissors, made a few fast cuts, and bingo!" She raised both arms and showed me.

"It looks good."

"At first I thought she didn't like me."

"Peggy didn't?"

Rachel nodded and pointed. There was Peggy about ten yards ahead, standing on a chair and waving to us.

"Where do you think she bought that outfit?" Rachel asked.

It looked like a man's checkered sport coat. As she waved again, it rose to reveal an expanse of white tights.

"Peggy's kind of a trendsetter," I explained. "She was written up in the paper and everything. She makes all that stuff herself."

"Where do you guys know her from, school?"

"She was a year ahead of us before she dropped out to take cosmetology classes. She's really good at that, too, I guess."

"But you all were in the same classes?"

I shook my head. "No."

"Did you ever go out with her?"

"Uh-uh."

"Do she and Sully go together?"

"No. I mean, they never have. It just kind of happened, how we got to be friends, I mean. One day Sully and I were walking across campus and Tommy Thompson and some other creeps were giving Peggy a hard time, pulling her clothes and stuff and calling her names."

"That was gallant," she said, smiling. "She was like a damsel in distress. Did you get in a fight and everything?"

"It didn't last long."

"It's funny," Rachel said. "I never knew one Peggy

before. Bradleyville's got two: this one and the one everybody writes about on the bathroom walls."

"That's Peggy. That's what the fight was about."

"Oh, God. The poor thing."

A band called Mojo opened. At first they seemed like just another bunch of guys with those dreadlocks that for all I know they put on in the dressing room.

But there was something spooky about them. The lead guitarist solemnly announced the titles: "Sad Forebodings of What Is Going to Happen." "The Open Window of Discontent." "The Dust We Love." "Landscape of the Hungry Ghosts." Not exactly your average rock concert.

They were pretty good, too, but I was a little distracted by trying to sway with the others so that nobody would think I was just woozy.

Then all of a sudden . . .

"I don't believe it," Rachel said. "That woman looks so much like my mom."

"Are you kidding? The guy in the sport coat looks like my dad. I mean, for a minute. . . ."

"Do you think they're together?" She leaned into me, grabbing my forearm like we were at the movies on Halloween.

"How weird!"

We watched them make their way toward the exit.

The guy really did resemble my father: the same thinning hair in front, the same thin lips. He was fairly good-looking, but I'd already begun to wonder if my hair would fall out while my lips shrunk.

"Do you know what I'd do," Rachel said thoughtfully, "in every town Dad and I would move to? I'd automatically make friends with all the other kids whose mom or dad had died. I didn't try. It just happened. It was like we could pick each other out. I remember this boy in Miami. We liked each other, you know? So after a little while he took me home to meet his folks, and there they are and there are all his brothers and sisters looking like they're never going to die and I thought, What does he need me for?" She turned to me, her eyes bigger and, if possible, sadder than ever. "Isn't that a funny thing to think?"

Spontaneously I reached for her hand. Amazingly, I didn't miss.

"I'm sixteen years old," she said, "and not a day goes by that I don't think about my mom or wonder when I'm going to . . ." Instead of finishing the sentence, she pointed to the hot lights that hung above us. I could see the insects that had flown too close. We sat in an intermittent rain of tiny bodies.

"C'mon. Let's dance," I said.

She pointed to the ushers. "Isn't it against the law or something?"

"It'll be okay."

It was against the law, but there weren't enough ushers in the world, and the performers didn't help. They all had this gorgeous accent, like tropical birds educated at Oxford, and they urged us, "Don't be fearful now. Let your spirits soar."

Luckily we were sitting on the aisle, so when a rent-a-cop came by, we just danced right back into our seats and then out again as he frantically tried to keep hundreds of people off their feet.

I danced like I had one foot nailed to the floor, but it didn't seem to matter. It was still fun, and Rachel started smiling a little, one of those brave smiles.

I don't know how it happened, but someone bumped up against me or her, throwing us within a few inches of each other, close enough for me to smell the perfume she was wearing and the Dentyne she was chewing, and then without even thinking about it, we were kissing.

We didn't use tongues or anything, but it was still awful nice. Rachel was a soft kisser, and she wrinkled her brow a little like she was concentrating real hard. Debbie had been a hard kisser with a kind of timer: after a little while her mouth popped open and stayed that way.

I liked this better.

It was late when I got home. We'd gone out to eat after the concert and then to an under-twenty-one club, where I'd danced with Rachel again, if you call standing in one spot and swaying like a tree dancing.

I waved goodbye to Sully, then just stood there in the dark for a few seconds. I was pretty sure I liked Rachel. I wondered if she liked me.

Then I tried my key, but the door was unlocked. Inside, my mom was sitting at the kitchen table having a glass of wine and reading a magazine. She smiled up at me, but I was stony. I had my values: no smiles for ax murderers, slobbering vivisectionists, or parents who turned on me.

"Did you have a good time?" she asked.

"It was okay."

I could see her switch on her Dishevelment Meter. Automatically I smoothed my hair and willed every wrinkle away.

"Honey," she said seriously, "I feel way out of my league doing this." She gestured as if describing the longest home run ever. "Way, way out. And for a lot of reasons I wish your dad were here to do it."

"I know what you're going to say, and I know plenty."

"About what?"

"About what you're going to ask about."

"Which is?"

"God, Mom. You know."

"I know I do. Do you?"

"Okay, okay. Sex, right?"

"I need to be certain, Walker."

"Just don't worry. I know all about it." I plunged both hands into my pockets like I was about to show her the rare coins of insight collected from dozens of books and a thousand bull sessions with Sully, the doctor's son. Then farther down would be the loose change of my halting chats with Dad.

"What did your father tell you, anyway?"

"A lot. Honest."

"I understand that," she said patiently, "but a lot in general or a lot in depth or —"

"A lot, that's all. Plenty. More than enough." I found myself spasmodically clenching my fists, which were still buried in my pockets. Until I imagined what that probably looked like. Quickly I tucked them under my arms like I was cold.

"Specifically," she said. "What did he tell you?" She put up a cautionary palm. "Not enough to embarrass you, but enough so that I can sleep nights."

"It was all in health ed., anyway: ovulation, menstrual periods, the never-to-be-forgotten drama of the sperm and the egg, masturbation, venereal disease . . ."

"But what," she insisted, "did your father say to you?"

"I'm not going to do anything wrong!"

"Honey, of course not. But since a lot of things about your father were a mystery to me, how do I know what he told you?"

I gestured helplessly. "About birth control, that's all."

"You know what condoms are, then?"

"Places you live that don't have yards?"

"Those are condos!"

"I know. I know. I was only kidding. This whole conversation makes me very nervous. I mean, I don't understand why you don't know what Dad told me. Didn't you guys communicate?"

"You haven't been listening to Dr. Phil again, have you?" she asked. Now she was trying to keep it light. "Didn't I tell you to only watch mindless violence?"

"Well, didn't you?"

"Your father may have worked for the phone company, but communication was not one of his gifts. He could have told you anything about sex. Or nothing. I never knew what he was thinking, or how much he knew about anything."

"But you two . . ." My mouth opened and closed. I looked like a hungry fish.

"Made love?"

This conversation was going from bad to worse. My stomach growled. There was that hunger again. Oh, for a Twinkie the size of a Ford.

"Okay, look," I said quickly. "He asked me if I knew about sex and I said yes."

"That was it?"

"Uh-huh."

"Where did this orgy of intimacy take place?"

"I don't remember, exactly — the mall, maybe."

"Your father told you about the facts of life in the mall?"

"What's the difference where he told me? He told

me; isn't that what you want to hear? And it took a long time, too. We talked a lot."

"Your father loved you, Walker, but he never talked a lot in his life. Now that he's gone, at least don't kid yourself. Whenever you wanted anything, you asked me, remember? Then I waited for the right moment and asked him. You couldn't do anything direct with your father, you know that. He was like some rare animal. If you rushed up to him yelling and waving your arms, he'd be gone in a flash. So I just tiptoed around until everything was just right and then I'd put my hand out and pet him. That's how I got your ten-speed, that's how I made it okay for you to use the car and to decorate your room with the Hottie of the Month."

"I took those down."

"It was always that way, sweetheart," she said relentlessly. "Don't pretend it was different."

I could feel the corners of my mouth turn down and start to quiver. "Why didn't you get a divorce if everything was so horrible?"

"But it wasn't."

"What'd you guys have in common, then? It sure wasn't long talks about who said what to your son."

She began to tick items off her list, snapping a finger up for each one. "We liked to travel and we did, especially before you were born. We liked to buy expensive wines and compare them. We both wanted to live close to a big city but not in it. We wanted to have one child, no more. We liked to cook . . ." She stopped to sigh.

"God, we had the nicest times in the kitchen, never saying a word — just chopping and grating and tasting. Your dad put fresh ginger in everything." She looked at me, her eyes misting over like windows in the winter. "I can't even keep it in the house anymore. And if I'm out somewhere and I smell it, I think my heart is just going to . . ." She stood up. "Well, I just have to leave, that's all."

The phone rang and we both looked toward the living room.

"Now, who can that be?" she said.

I waited to see if it could possibly be for me, maybe Sully with some midnight insight, then I heard Mom say, "Oh, hi," so I looked in the refrigerator and scarfed about half a package of cheese and some leftover pizza.

Boy, it was sure getting strange around the house, all those secrets coming out. It made me feel weird to realize that I didn't really know my dad. Who had I loved? And who did I miss? It was like that old quiz show he used to watch on cable, the one where people lied about who they were. Will the real father please stand up?

"It was Wanda," Mom said. "She's got the flu for sure and wants me to come in a little early tomorrow night."

"Wanda?"

"The Wildcat. I don't know why I have to be early just because she's sick."

"Wanda the *Wildcat*?"

"Look," Mom said brusquely. "I started this talk so I could be sure that when you decide to make love with someone you'll know everything you need in order to make careful and considerate choices." She took one of my hands in hers. "Okay? Does that make sense?"

"I guess. It just sounds funny coming from a stripper." I'm afraid I pretty much spit out the last word.

Just before, my mom and I had been like two ice cubes left out in the sink, slowly melting, slowly trickling toward each other. Then bam! Right back in the freezer.

Mom sighed. I looked down at my shoes. Of course I should have apologized, but I couldn't seem to get the words out.

She turned back to her magazine; I was about to escape to my room.

"Just a minute. Remember this?" She held the lawyer's letter at arm's length, head back, nose in the air. "I want you to look this land over, and I want you to do it tomorrow."

"God, what do I know about —"

"Go look at it. Make sure there's not an oil well out there that we don't know about. Just do what your father used to do."

Well, I thought, maybe it wouldn't be so bad after all. I could call Rachel; maybe she'd ride out with me.

"And don't call your little girlfriend, either, at least not now. It's late and you'll wake up her parents."

"She doesn't have parents," I said. "She's like me."

"Half an orphan? Poor baby. When do I get to meet this foundling?"

"I don't know. It's not like you're home all the time, is it?"

Boy, who knows where those crappy sentences come from? Right out of nowhere. And then they're out and it's too late.

Mom took a swallow of her wine, stared out the window, and sighed again, heavier this time. I just stood there feeling like a lot less than two cents. Then I turned and went up the hall to my room.

After a few minutes I thought that I should just go back out to the kitchen and tell Mom I was sorry, but I didn't. So I hoped that she would come to the door, knock softly, and tell me that she was quitting to become the manager of a candy plant.

I lay there waiting for the obviously impossible. All I

heard was the water running, the toilet flushing, the ghostly crawl of her slippers on the green carpet, and the sound of her door closing.

"We saw you at the concert, Walkman. Are you getting into that new girl's designer jeans?"

It was Tommy Thompson, lurking outside the cafeteria with his henchmen. Tommy was good-looking, if you like those Hitler Youth types. And his father was rich. So girls just naturally ran after him.

But he could be a real jerk, too, as Peggy could have testified. Seeing him with his buddies was like looking at an exhibition in the natural history museum: The Stages of Man. At the top was Tommy — blond and clear-eyed, the ultimate predator. Then there were the intermediate stages: Vince Babbit and Tony DeLong, guys who slumped a lot and sometimes had trouble getting the wrapper off a Snickers. And at the bottom was Art Forney. Built like a big toe, he always breathed through his mouth and looked like he cut his own hair with broken glass.

"Chain your bodyguards," I said. "Let's just you and me, Thompson."

I knew he'd never do it.

"Where's your boyfriend Sully, you fat faggot?"

Sticks and stones. In one sentence I'm plundering

Rachel and in the next bisexual, at least. What an all-round guy.

Tommy and I naturally gave each other the finger and that was that. I began to look for Rachel, but didn't run into her until after sixth period. We saw each other at the same time and both of us waved big slow waves like we were underwater. As usual she was dressed up and then some. If we'd been Indians, her name would have been Many Clothes. And mine? He Who Lives In Pantry.

"I had a nice time the other night," she said, hugging her books to her breasts, or where her breasts probably were. Her sweater was decorated with a tic-tac-toe grid and there were two huge *O*'s in just about the right place.

"I was wondering," I began, but stopped short when she turned to wave at someone and shout, "C-plus if I'm lucky." Then she apologized immediately.

"I'm sorry, Walker, I'm a little hyper. School can make me really nervous."

"I was going to ask if you'd drive out and look at this land my dad left me. You being a developer's daughter and all, I thought maybe you could give me some advice."

"About what?"

"Whatever," I said lamely.

"Today?" She leaned, looking for her watch, which was partly lost among books and folders.

"It wouldn't take long. I mean, what's out there? Dirt, right?"

"I was sort of planning to go to the mall. And then I've got to run some errands for my dad."

"What if we went to the mall together first and then on out to the other side of town?"

"You'd go to Westgate with me?" she asked happily. "I thought you didn't like malls."

"I haven't been in a long time. Maybe it's changed. Or maybe I was wrong."

It's funny how people can't simply tell each other the truth. I just wanted to see Rachel and be with her. Why didn't I say that?

Were we already like my mom and dad, who didn't communicate unless they were cooking? Or was this communication, after all, like in English class where you looked underneath the cold words on the page to find the warm ones?

When we got to the Saturn, Rachel patted the dashboard and said, "This is okay."

"What is?"

"Your car."

"My mom's car, you mean."

"It's nice."

"Your nose is going to grow."

"Well, I've never been in one like it."

"You could say that about a wheelbarrow."

"I don't care about cars and stuff like that."

I was glad for that bit of news.

"Give me a minute by myself, okay?" Immediately she started doing some kind of breathing exercises, huffing and puffing. I looked around, grateful that none of the other kids could see. Maybe Debbie hadn't been the most stimulating companion in history, but she at least breathed like a normal person and not the Big Bad Wolf.

"I went to a stress clinic once," she explained. "I guess almost nobody gets enough oxygen."

"Too bad you can't just eat oxygen; I'd always have enough."

She grinned and began to pant again, then stopped abruptly. "Sully's pretty smart, isn't he?"

"Brilliant, I guess. When we started high school, we took all these tests and he did some unheard-of thing like getting everything right. The teachers all but put up a shrine."

"I feel really out of it in these accelerated classes."

"It must be hard going from school to school like you do."

"I didn't mind moving, at least not at first." She turned to me, pressing one invisible breast against the torn upholstery. "Did I tell you how my mom died?"

I shook my head.

"Shopping. Can you believe it? It turns out she had this congenital heart problem that nobody knew about. It made me think that if she had it, maybe I had it, too, and I'd just die sometime without ever being sick or anything. It made me want to not wait for anything, so after Mom passed away, Dad started his own company and we traveled. I'm sixteen and I've been to London and Rome and I've lived in New York and Miami and Santa Barbara. I've done just about everything a girl my age can do."

"Okay," I said soothingly. "I believe you."

"Sorry. Look, would it be okay if we didn't talk for a little bit? I can calm myself down sometimes if I just sit still and imagine some really pretty place."

Had just talking made her that nervous or was it something I'd done? Jesus, at this rate I'd have to call the 24-Hour Crisis Hot Line.

"I can't decide," she said, opening her eyes and frowning, "whether to vizualize Peachtree Plaza or Ghirardelli." She turned to me eagerly. "Dad and I were in San Francisco last year, and we got to go to Ghirardelli way before it opened. God, Walker, it was gorgeous." Then she nodded her head decisively. "That's it, then. California, here I come."

As I drove and she breathed evenly beside me, I had

a little meditation of my own. She'd said, "I've done just about everything a girl my age can do." Did that mean she wasn't a virgin? And what if she wasn't? And what if she was? Would I like her less? More?

I knew how Sully felt. He had to marry a beautiful girl who had been reared by nuns, one stamped for approval by his father. She also had to be sexy out of her mind but attracted only to him, like a laser that scorched his bedroom, leaving the rest of the neighborhood intact.

I wasn't exactly sure how I felt. Everyone knew it was okay for girls to want to make love and even to want to as much as boys. Everyone said so: Oprah, Dr. Ruth, even Dear Abby.

So it was okay, but was Rachel like that? Just because it was okay didn't mean everybody had to be that way.

Was I like that? I was horny all the time, but with Debbie, neither of us had seriously considered going to bed together. We'd just kissed for a few weeks and then, with her gripping my one hand with both of hers like she was holding back a poisoned dagger, I'd touched her breast. But that was it; that was the little dance we did.

Still, that was a long time ago, almost a year. I'd only been fifteen then. For adults, a year or two can't mean that much. At thirty-seven a person is just about the same as he was at thirty-five. But at sixteen, a kid is nothing like the fourteen-year-old he was. He's outgrown all his clothes again, cut his hair five different ways, and changed his mind a thousand times.

I guess I'd known who I was back in the Dark Ages of Early Adolescence, but who was I now? And who was this girl beside me?

We crossed the crowded parking lot hand in hand like Jack and Jill, strolling along like the asphalt was a country road and the concrete steps a grassy slope. Once inside the big doors, Rachel took a deep breath, opening her arms like someone greeting the sunrise. She had on a mostly black outfit and looked like a Druid.

"Isn't it great?" she asked.

"Who builds these things, anyway?"

"Developers." She'd wandered over to the railing and was looking down on the first level. "You and I could build if we had the money and the concept and the zoning. C'mon."

She held out one hand but when I reached, she'd moved, so she caught my wrist. We walked that way for a few yards, acting, I guess, like we'd planned it. I wondered if anybody would think I'd been nabbed for shoplifting, or worse, that I needed to be led everywhere because my IQ was smaller than my waist size.

She inhaled deeply. "Doesn't it smell just great?"

"If you like caramel corn and polyester."

"I know. And perfume and leather and . . ."

"You really like this place, don't you?"

"Walker, I swear to God, I love it. Don't you?"

"I don't think so."

"All I know is, a mall can really mellow me out. Who needs Valium when you've got all this."

"I took Valium once," I said. "Right after my dad died. I couldn't seem to get to sleep, so my mom started giving me some of hers."

"I know; me too." She let go of my wrist so that she could use her hands to cover her face for an instant.

"C'mon," I said. "Let's talk about something else."

She nodded bravely. "Are you hungry?"

"No," I lied.

"Me neither. Let's sit a minute."

"Don't you want to buy something?"

"No." She looked surprised. "Do you?"

"You mean you just come out here . . ."

She finished for me. "To be here? Sure."

Below us was a sea of hats, bald spots, and hair. We leaned over the railing, our elbows touching.

"People don't look kind of dead to you?" I asked.

"Nope."

"And you don't feel claustrophobic?"

She pointed up. "Skylights."

"Well, it all just makes me want to get my hands dirty."

"You know," she said thoughtfully, "when I finally saw Disneyland a few years ago, I was really disappointed. I mean, I've walked up perfect streets all my life. What did Sleeping Beauty's castle mean to me compared to Lord and Taylor?"

Right on cue a maintenance man in pressed coveralls stopped nearby to pick up a gum wrapper.

"Can you wait," she said abruptly, "while I go to the bathroom?"

I watched her walk away, wondering, frankly, what her legs looked like under those enormous pants. It was almost summer and she was completely covered up. I had better undress her soon; once winter came it would take hours just to get all her clothes off.

A lot of kids were with their parents, and I couldn't help but think about being here with my dad. He was shopping for the running shoes that would carry him into the path of that Pontiac. I couldn't look at some kid with his dad's arm around his shoulders without feeling lonely and a little weird. Not that my dad had put his arm around my shoulders that day. Or any day, actually. He wasn't touchy-feely like my mom. But we'd walked side by side and talked about the mall and about how it'd been built on land that he had once worked on, driving a tractor for some old farmer and getting paid two dollars an hour.

Thinking about that made me so hungry I got a

stomach cramp. I stood up and stretched, trying to concentrate on something else so that Rachel didn't find me doubled up on the spotless tiles alternately weeping and calling for a double cheeseburger.

Right below me four or five employees, dressed in jeans, straw hats, and checkered shirts, were handing out free pieces of sausage. They had straw in their socks and cuffs, like scarecrows. From the store right behind them came square-dance music, but the Muzak was oozing either Mozart or Three Dog Night. I began to feel strange again.

Turning, I spotted Rachel talking to a salesgirl. They wore the exact same outfit, and in the store window stood their catatonic sister. That didn't help my emotional state either.

"The Garden of Gardner," Rachel said, slipping in beside me, "is going to have three thousand bathrooms if I have anything to say about it."

"Can we go?"

"Are you okay?"

"Sure," I said, like all real men when they're only shot through the brain. "I just have to get the car home, and I want to get to the other side of town first, and . . ."

"Yeah, me too. I told my dad I'd eat with him tonight for sure."

We drove slowly along the frontage road, trying to make sense of the map that lawyer had given my mother. Everything was rich and green, all the farmland in every direction, even the ditches and the sides of the road had things coming up with all their might.

Then we came to a big section with hardly anything growing at all. I checked the map. Sure enough.

Rachel and I climbed out and surveyed the place.

"Gee," I said. "This looks awful."

She eyed it shrewdly. "You've got access; that's what counts."

"Access to what?"

"Your place borders the highway. It's like riverfront property; it's the best, that's all."

"But why is it so sad-looking? If this was a person I'd just inherited, I'd buy him a new suit and a hot meal."

Just then someone across the way wearing overalls and an honest-to-God straw hat cut the engine on his tractor, climbed down, stepped over the broken-down barbed wire that separated our two fields, and began to slowly make his way toward us.

Rachel eyed the uneven ground. "Do you think he needs help or something?"

"Probably, but I'll bet he wouldn't take it."

"Name's Kramer," he said, taking off his hat for Rachel's sake.

We introduced ourselves, and I explained what we were doing out there. Then I asked what had happened to my land.

"Mostly it got leased to some chuckleheaded bastards who read the stock market page once and if soybeans was up, they planted soybeans first thing in the morning. Then they planted them next time and the time after that, too. Pretty soon the ground gets tired, like if somebody came along every night for a week and took a pint or so of your blood, you'd get tired, too. Probably your daddy didn't know what was going on, but maybe that ain't much of an excuse, either."

I pointed. "What are you growing over there?"

"Nothing. It's called green manure. You just let it grow, then plow it back under. You have to put back what you took out — that's all there is to it. It's just good business."

"You mean all that green stuff isn't anything?" Rachel asked.

"No, it's oats. I only meant it wasn't no crop to harvest and sell."

"So what goes in there next year that you can harvest and sell?"

74

"Not a blessed thing. By the time next year comes that land might be miles of asphalt and women with fat ankles and nothing to do all day but go into stores and say, 'My, but ain't the air-conditioning nice.'"

"So what are you going to do?" I asked.

"Sell. Probably can't afford not to."

"Did they offer you a lot of money for your land?"

"Not a thing yet. But they will, sooner or later. Everybody knows this is where the new mall's going to go. Don't you worry about the price, either. They've got to come to you; you've got access. You're sittin' in the catbird seat, son."

I said that I didn't know why, exactly, but I felt bad about my property and in a funny way I wished there was something I could do.

Kramer pounced right on me. "There is," he said, "unless you're just moving your lips to hear yourself talk. I've got more seed than I can ever use and it won't be much use once they get serious about building out here. So I'll give it to you."

"What seed?" But he wasn't about to slow down.

"You can use that little Farmall Cub of mine, too, if you'll just pay for the gas, and that goes for just about anything else I've got that you might need, including an old Oliver Sixty with a seven-foot double disc if you get to feeling high and mighty."

He was pretty fired up, and Rachel took a step closer to me.

"What would I need all that for?"

"To plant yourself some oats, that's what. Make this place look like something."

"Oats?" I said.

"Like Quaker oats?" asked Rachel, and I pictured the round package with the happy fat man on the front.

"The very same. It wouldn't take long, neither."

"Planting wouldn't?"

"Plowing, planting, cultivating. Hell, it's only forty acres. I used to do ten times that with two field hands and a horse-drawn plow."

I waved my hands helplessly. "I don't know how to drive a tractor."

"Can you drive a car?"

I pointed to my mom's Saturn.

"Stick shift?"

"My dad taught me on a stick shift."

"Then you just wait right here and I'll bring her around."

"Listen, it's late. Maybe we should . . ."

But he was already on his way.

Mr. Kramer motioned for me to climb into the Farmall's palm-shaped seat, which seemed to hang between the two huge rear wheels. He pointed to everything, and touched what he could reach.

"Now, this here's the clutch and the brake. Throttle's up here and that's the gearshift. Happy landings."

Sitting there on the throbbing machine, I wiped both hands on my doily-colored pants and read the gear pattern on the knob. I looked at Mr. Kramer and mimed, "What now?"

His hand described a big circle and he came closer to shout, "Just get the feel of her."

Swallowing hard, I wrestled it into first, held the throttle like I was strangling a viper, and eased the clutch out.

The tractor jumped about a foot and died.

"Well, that wasn't so hard," I said in the sudden silence. "Am I done plowing?"

"Crank her up and try again."

Another foot.

"Better call your dad, Rachel. At this rate we won't get home till Christmas."

His thumb depressed an invisible starter, so I put mine on the real one and, lo and behold, actually got moving. Mr. Kramer bisected the circle to shout, "Little less throttle and let your clutch out all the way."

I went all the way around a couple of times, then made a figure eight or two. It was fun. The steering

wheel seemed to connect directly with the wide front
end. When I turned the black plastic an inch or two, I
was pointed in another direction. It made my mom's car
seem like a big, soft toy.

"It'll feel different dragging a plow, but you'll adjust."

"When do we get started?"

"Why don't you meet me at my place about five-thirty."

"Gee, my mom's got to have the car by five-thirty."

"A.M., son. That's in the morning."

"I'd give a lot to be like him," Rachel said, waving one
last time at the disappearing tractor.

"Like Mr. Kramer? Why?"

"Do you know what you want to do when you
grow up?"

I shook my head. "Not really."

"See? But every day Mr. Kramer gets up, feeds the
cows, does some chores — it sounds like heaven."

"Maybe he doesn't want to, though; maybe he has to."

"Then how about Sully? Hasn't he known what he's
wanted to do ever since he was a little kid?"

"More or less. His father . . ."

"Traveling is fun, but a person just can't travel all her
life and put down *traveler* on her income-tax form where it
asks for occupation. I still change my mind every day. I

want to be a psychologist sometimes — can you imagine that? And then I want to go to New York and work."

"Doing what?"

"I don't know; that's the trouble. And then I start thinking about all the poor people in the world and I want to do something."

"Like give them all checking accounts."

She leaned toward me. "I don't understand why I'm young and rich and they're poor and starving. Do you ever feel apologetic? I want to apologize to people sometimes. I want to say, 'I'm sorry I'm the way I am and you're the way you are, but it's not my fault. It just happened.'" She sat back dispiritedly. "I'd really like to do something, though, to help people or to make the world a better place."

"People like the places your dad builds; does that count?"

"Oh, I guess. But it's not like I do anything but spend about a zillion dollars a year buying clothes so I can look like everybody else."

"Well, there's no shops here — not yet, anyway. So let's take a little walk before the escalators go in."

We rocked on the uneven earth, laughing and bouncing off one another. Halfway across I stopped and murmured, "My land."

"What?" She was breathing a little hard.

"I said, 'My land.'" Then I made my voice as low as possible and tried it again. "My land." I turned to Rachel. "It really is kind of a magical phrase. I say it and get goose bumps."

She sang the first line of an old folk song: "This land is your land, this land is my land . . ." Her voice was sweet and airy.

"This earth is mine," I said firmly. "You varmints get off my land."

"Land ho," she ventured.

"Give me land, lots of land under starry skies above."

"The fat of the land."

"Easy now. Don't get personal."

"You're not fat. You just have big bones."

"Big bones covered with fat."

"I'm a little hippy," she said softly.

"Well, then this relationship is doomed, because I'm a big Republican."

She laughed politely and patted herself on the bottom.

"That's why I like these new fashions. They cover me up."

"You look fine to me."

"How can you tell? I'm always bundled up like an only child with a cold."

I thought it was great of her to tell me those things

and not sound destructive. I was self-critical beyond belief. For example, I wanted a different nose, a thinner one, so I'd squeeze the one I had until it was sore and generally give it a hard time. But when Rachel talked, she sounded like her own best friend: realistic, maybe, but not mean. Me, I was my own worst enemy.

We sat down under an enormous oak, a few yards into Mr. Kramer's property but facing mine. I felt like Adam looking out the front door of Eden: here it was rich and sweet and moist. There it was strictly sweat-of-thy-brow.

Rachel settled back against the trunk. "It was really nice of your father to leave you this place," she said.

"Yeah, but stuff's been coming up about him lately that I can't believe."

"You too? I'm still learning things about my mom. Not bad things," she added quickly. "But she didn't like yogurt and she wouldn't give to charities." She raised one hand in exasperation. "I didn't know that until last week. And then my dad told me they'd talked about getting a divorce once."

"Adults have all kinds of secrets, I guess. I don't think I have any." *What about your mother, the exotic dancer?* said a little voice right down by my solar plexus. "Or at least not very many," I added feebly. Then, before she could ask me what those were, I said, "Do you think it's silly of me to want to work this place?"

"I think it's nice. Honest."

"What good does it do, though? Who does it help? I'm not exactly going to ship the grain to Africa."

"Mr. Kramer said your dad didn't know any better than to lease to people who would use up all the vitamins and nitrogen and stuff. Maybe you just want to put things right." She looked right into my eyes. "You're a nice person, Walker. This is just the kind of thing you'd do." She sighed and closed her eyes, resting against the oak.

I didn't know what to say, but I did know that I wanted to kiss her. I leaned across; with her eyes closed she couldn't see me coming.

"It's so peaceful out here," she said, right into my nose like it was a microphone or something.

I was frozen, worse than a deer nailed to the road by headlights. God, if she opened her eyes and saw me two inches away, she would probably scream and shoot up the tree like a squirrel.

"Don't move," I whispered.

She stiffened. "What?"

"There's a bug in your hair."

"How big?"

What a rational girl. "You know how big a pancake is?" I'd retreated gracefully, so when her eyes flew open everything seemed normal.

82

"I've got a bug on me that's as big as a pancake?"

"No. That's just for comparison. It's about one-thousandth the size of a —"

She brushed at her short dark hair. "Oh, he won't hurt anything." Then she looked at me and leaned forward. Either she wanted to be kissed or she'd become addicted to chatting with my nostrils.

"Have you kissed a lot of girls?" she asked softly.

"No."

"Me neither. Boys, I mean. Naturally. But at the concert the other night you seemed so"— she searched for a word —"polished."

Now we were so close that when she smiled her teeth were as enormous and white as the cleanest wash on any TV ad.

"I didn't feel very polished."

"My mother told me that kissing well was a highly desirable quality in a man. She said a lot of other things wax and wane but kissing was forever."

Boy, I really wished she hadn't drawn attention to it. I was like the perfectly natural pitcher who goes to training camp, gets his delivery analyzed, and then can't hit the backstop behind home plate.

As she leaned even closer with her lips parted and slightly moist, I wondered if mine were moist enough; I wondered if they were soft like hers, and if they weren't, how I could make them soft again.

Quickly I slipped my hand up to check. They felt okay. I knew I couldn't keep her waiting like that forever, so I just plunged ahead, adjusting all the time, everything from prim old lady to doctor-examines-tonsils. I must have looked like a hallucinating halibut.

She didn't seem to notice; she just leaned into me, putting one hand up to gently touch my face.

I might have stopped right there and told her the truth about what I wanted to do with my life. I wanted to go where the kissing never stopped. I know how terrible and selfish this sounds, but I didn't want to help people or make their lives better. I probably wouldn't even have saved somebody from drowning unless she would have rewarded me with more kisses.

Rachel and I necked — as my mother still called it — in a kind of Morse code: long dashes of kissing followed by sharp little smackers, then long ones again. I was content. In a way I was even glad not to knead and probe like the witch in "Hansel and Gretel."

Of course I wanted to do more, too, but I barely knew Rachel. If I ever touched her all over and took her clothes off and made love to her, it would not be today.

"God," she said, stretching luxuriously, "this is really nice. Don't you just want to stay here forever?"

"Oh, my God," I said, and I sat up straight, leaving Rachel gasping and flushed.

"Will she be mad?" Rachel asked, looking at herself in the rearview mirror.

"No." I pressed on the accelerator. "There's plenty of time."

"God, I can't meet your mother looking like this. I've got dirt all over my pants. She'll think I fall down all the time."

Meet my mother? I pictured her standing on the steps, tapping her foot, tassels jingling angrily. Rachel would scream in horror and embarrassment; she would never see me again. She would tell everyone in school. Nobody would go out with me. The story would follow me to college and I would live in a tiny, spider-infested room by myself for four years.

Instead, there she was in her black slacks and her red blouse, looking like she'd just gotten back from the ground round sale at Kroger's.

"I didn't know whether to worry or get mad," she said when we followed her inside. "Now that you're all right, I can get mad."

"We were talking to this old farmer out at the land Dad bought for me, and we kind of lost track of time."

She scrutinized us. "This old farmer, huh?"

Rachel looked down at her shoes.

"I'm Walker's mother," Mom said, holding out her hand.

"We didn't mean to make you late, Mrs. Davis."

"I'm not mad at you."

"Talking to Mr. Kramer really was interesting."

"If you say so." Mom had that I-know-what-you've-been-up-to look on her face. She picked up her big, soft purse. "Well, I have to go, or they'll be banging their glasses on the table."

"What do you do?" Rachel asked politely.

I jumped right in. "Waitress," I said.

My mother and I looked at each another; it was one of those significant glances you hear so much about. I wondered if she was disappointed in me.

"Can I drop you somewhere?" Mom asked Rachel.

"That'd be great. Do you go by the high school? My car's there."

"I'll ride along," I said, afraid of what they would talk about. Couldn't you just hear the conversation?

> RACHEL: *(politely)* And where do you
> work as a waitress, Mrs. Davis?

MOM: Hey, I'm not a waitress, kiddo.
I'm a stripper.
RACHEL: *(screaming)* Let me out!
Let me out of here. Help! Police!

"That's okay," Rachel said. "This way your mom and I can get to know each other."

"No, no, no, no, no." I sounded like a machine gun.

"Honey," my mother said, looking at me with those eyes the same color as mine. "I wouldn't. Honest."

Rachel inspected us both. Poor thing — she was like a tourist who didn't speak the language.

"Bye, Walker. See you at school, okay?"

I put out my hand and she shook it.

"Today was fun," she said. Then she squeezed. Meaningfully.

Immediately I got a killer erection. I'm surprised I didn't turn pale as yogurt, because all the blood in my body must have rushed to my shorts.

Woozy with desire, I watched them from the kitchen window. Then I walked into the living room. It occurred to me that I'd never been alone with a girl in my own house. The place seemed big and mysterious, and every hall led to a bedroom. I wondered if my bed was made. Even if it was, so what? Did you say to a girl, "Want to see how well I made my bed?" Fat chance.

I could hear the furnace hum and the refrigerator go on and off. Was this what it was like to be married to someone, to live in a huge house with bedrooms everywhere and to be able to go into any of them anytime you wanted?

I have to admit that I felt very grown-up as I sauntered around the house. My house. My flat. My place.

Then I went into the bathroom and jerked off like mad.

I was standing in the spotless kitchen wiping the last saucepan when Mom came home from work.

"A little obvious," she said, "but still nice."

Boy, she saw right through me. "It's not a big deal," I said. "I just need the car at five-thirty, that's all, and only for a couple of hours."

"You know better than that, Walker. I have to be at the club by six."

"In the morning. Five-thirty in the morning."

"What in the world are you going to do at that hour?"

I filled in the details, scrupulously wiping a dish like one of those guys in the commercials.

"But why," she asked, "plant anything if the land's just going to be sold?"

"We don't know when, though. And if it's a long time, I'll have these oats."

"Which you plow under."

I stacked the dinner plates perfectly. Now if the camera would just zoom in, I could turn around and scream how clean everything was. "Right, so there's stuff down there next year."

"Oh, well, stuff. Why didn't you say so."

"It's like vitamins. Mr. Kramer calls it green manure."

"You grow manure?"

"Look, it's more or less Dad's fault the land is so tired. I just want to put things right, that's all. It's no skin off your ass."

"Watch it, buster."

"Nose, then. Mom, I'll do all the work. What little bit it costs I'll take out of my savings."

Her voice dropped a couple of octaves and she went soft around the eyes. "You don't feel very well taken care of, do you? So you want to take care of something else."

"You sound like Sully. The point is, what's the difference? God knows it's harmless. It's not like I was asking to borrow the car to rob banks."

"What does Rachel think about all this Farmer Brown business, anyway?"

"She likes it. She said it was nice of me to want to do it."

"By the way, Walker." She paused to pour herself a glass of wine from the tall bottle in the refrigerator.

I got ready for the bad news. I've never heard an

adult start anything good with "By the way." Never "By the way, here's your new Corvette." Or "By the way, could you use an extra two hundred dollars for lunch?"

"I don't want you and Rachel here by yourselves when I'm at work. I don't know what her folks would think, but . . ."

"Her folk. Her mother died."

"I'm sorry. I don't know what her father would think, but even if he drove her over himself and dropped her off with an overnight bag, I don't want it. Understood?"

I said I did. "What about . . ."

She made a small circle in the center of the kitchen. "On the other hand, if you're going to park somewhere and get hit over the head by a maniac, come back here." She raised both hands. "God, what am I saying?"

"If we park and there's a big sign saying Maniac Area, we won't stay."

She had her hand to her forehead like The Great Mind-o about to predict, but the corners of her mouth were turned down and her chin was quivering. "God, you're really growing up, aren't you?"

"Am I grown-up enough to use the car to work with Mr. Kramer?"

"You're not going to let me play this out, are you?" she asked good-naturedly. "You're not even willing to let me do just a few minutes of Mom-in-Distress."

"Bribe me. Tell me I can have the —"

"Okay. But I get to cry, and"— she jumped on the *and* —"I get to put my arms around you."

A little later, when Mom was in the shower, I tried to call Rachel, but all I got was the machine saying Mr. Gardner wasn't home. Gardner. Some name for a guy who covered the earth with concrete.

Then I collapsed on my bed — right on top of Batman and Robin the Boy Wonder.

As I lay there, I felt completely sixteen. Nearly grown. Well, I'd sure had plenty of maturing experiences: my father had passed away, I'd been disappointed in love, my mother wasn't the person I'd thought she was at all. (Oh, and I had a driver's license and I'd been in a couple of really hairy fights.)

But I was still a virgin, so I felt like a picture of a man with a part missing.

Was Rachel going to be the one? Did she want to be? And what would I do if she did? God, no wonder I didn't want the kissing to stop. I wouldn't know what to do next.

Rachel might know, but would she want to show me? I was pretty sure girls wanted the guy to be in charge. And even if she didn't mind being the leader, how would I go about asking, "Uh, pardon me, miss. But where exactly does this go?"

Then the next thing I knew, the alarm was going off. Pitch black: *there must be some mistake.*

At the end of the dark lanes that left the slopy blacktop, beyond the billboards advertising Jesus and fertilizer, I could see the lights in farmhouses, outbuildings, and barns.

When I pulled into the yard, the tractor was already sitting out. The screen door opened and Mr. Kramer waved at me.

"Coffee?"

I shook my head as he came and leaned in the window.

"You're sure now? I've got fresh cream, and I mean fresh." He gestured toward the barn. "Years ago my oldest boy raised a scramble calf to about half a ton, and got a second for fat and form the next spring at the Saint Charles Fair. Bossy here is a great-great-great-granddaughter."

"Bossy?" I felt like I'd stepped into a coloring book.

"Maybe it'll wake you up to drive. You climb on up there and take the lead. I'll come along behind in the car so nobody smacks you in the rear end. No one's up and around at this time of the morning but darn fools like you and me, anyway."

The tractor didn't seem so unfamiliar; I even found

the switch for the headlamps and the fist-size taillights perched on top of the fenders right beside me.

I got started, killed the engine once, eased down the lane with ruts probably as old as I was, got onto the macadam, and gave it some gas.

I stood up to steer, like a sea captain. The sun was barely over the edge of the world; the air was cool, silky as a parachute, and it smelled wonderful.

Then we got to Paltry Acres. I sat, leaning on the dark, scarred wheel. Toward the edges — the road at my right, a fence and barrow ditch to the left — a few weeds had taken hold in a scaled-down version of plenty.

Mr. Kramer came up beside me, laying his hand on the smooth fender as if it were the solid rump of some animal. He held out his other hand palm-down, blessing-style, and sighted along it.

"It lays well enough," he said, "but it does look peaked."

"I'll bet even pigs wouldn't live here."

"Pigs," he said scornfully. "You even see a pig, kick it. It's either out, been out, or thinking about getting out."

"Well, what's the plan?"

"First tractor I had," he said softly, "came with high steel tires with lugs. I wasn't allowed to take it on the county roads."

I turned to look down at him. He was more at home then than now.

"Mattie and I had the sweetest little driving mare. She carried us all over the country." He slapped the fender rhythmically. Maybe he was listening to that mare's hooves or clucking to her. Maybe he was patting the slim thigh that lay beside his as he drove with one hand.

"Well, now," he said abruptly. "Tell you what. Let's start with a good-size piece but nothing too ambitious. Drive on up there to the line fence yonder, then come all the way back past me in a big circle. Go ahead and put the near side of the blade right up against where you've been. Then follow yourself around and around till you end up right in the center."

"Just like a big bull's-eye? I guess I imagined I'd just go back and forth."

"If it ever rains good, straight plowing's not the thing for this place, at least not right now. If you want, you could contour like so." He snaked his hand through the air, which was warming up in a hurry.

"No, the circle appeals to me."

"Then run on out there a ways and I'll show you how to set this little plow."

There was a long handle — the kind that I'd seen on cartoon steam shovels — that raised or lowered the staggered blades.

"Once you get the hang of it, set this about as low as she'll go."

"I guess I can't do it wrong, huh?" The handle was already damp with anxiety.

"Not with this place, son. Not now, anyways. Remember, when you get a good bite, give her some throttle."

"Okay." I wiped both palms on my silly flowered shirt.

"Oh, and one more thing." He stepped up beside me and took off his hat. "Get yourself one of these."

"It's still dark."

"Not for long."

I eased away, tugged on the handle, felt the blades go in, killed the engine. Mr. Kramer didn't even bother to turn around.

It was sure different pulling something, and my first hundred yards ranged from a few inches deep to a few feet. Sweat ran in my eyes and stung as I half sat in the springy seat, turning this way and that to see where I was going, where I'd been, and what kind of trajectory I'd left behind.

But I got the hang of it, and I could tell as the morning wore on how the soil changed. The farther I got from the line fences and the more I closed in on the bull's-eye, the easier it seemed, and I dismounted more and more often to let the blades down as far as they would go.

It was hot out there, even at eight A.M., and it was

95

dirty. The wind just picked up the soil and plastered it to me, but I loved it, lost on an island of noise.

I could see Mr. Kramer leaning against a tree, and every third or fourth time around he'd lift a finger in acknowledgment. Then I'd pass him, swing up over a tiny rise, and I'd be alone with the baked earth in front of me, and behind me the huge doodles I'd drawn.

chapter **3**

High school is just amazing. The government should copy its communications system, completely wireless and completely foolproof. What I mean is that everybody knew that Rachel and I liked each other. When I found her in the hall, she was talking to a bunch of kids, and they just melted away like ice on an iron. Only Sully stayed, but he was my best friend, so that was okay. The rules are complicated, but everybody knows them. Even Rachel, and she hadn't been at my school for more than two weeks. It must be somewhere in the gene pool or the DNA. Someday some scientist is going to discover it under his ultrapowerful microscope, a micro-teensy pamphlet right there in the smallest nucleus of the smallest atom: *How to Act in High School.*

"Walker," she said, shaking her head in mild exasperation. "Look at your hands."

They were a little dirty in places. "I guess I was in a hurry."

Rachel shifted her enormous bag with her initials sewn on it, came up with a perfumed towelette wrapped in foil, and began to rub at my fingers and palms. "You're worse than my father," she said happily.

Sully said he had to take a test. We watched him walk away. Rachel turned to me, smiling.

"What happened to your eyes?" I asked. "They're green today."

One hand went up to cover them, like a little girl who was "it" and counting to a hundred.

"I've got these different-colored contacts, is all; I change to match my outfits."

"You wear glasses?"

"Does it matter?"

"Well, I just didn't know the girl I like can't see her feet without prescription lenses."

"I was pretty sure you liked me," she said softly.

"I thought about you a lot while I was plowing this morning. It's magical out there, Rachel. I'm just all by myself, and when the sun comes up, it's like it's for only me. Except that I wish you were there."

"On your tractor?"

"I know our language is new to you, but in Bradleyville we call it a lap."

She blushed and looked delighted.

"Let's go out tonight, okay?"

"Walker, these accelerated classes are killing me. How about Friday?"

"Gee," I said seriously. "I'm busy Friday." I meant it as a joke but she looked so disappointed I couldn't finish. "No, I'm not. I was just kidding. Friday's fine."

"Really? You aren't just saying that?"

Rachel was wearing an enormous cardigan. Somehow when she leaned toward me, one of the books she held against her chest slipped down into it.

"Oh, God. There goes *The Great Gatsby.*"

She lifted one leg gracefully, trying to shift the other books back into a stack.

"Could you . . . ?" She gestured with her head toward her chest. "It's in there somewhere."

Gingerly I put my hand inside. I could feel some ribs. Under her blouse her body was warm and firm.

"Down more, I think."

"You city girls are shameless."

"Did you find it?" she whispered.

We were very close together and my blood was starting to percolate.

"Unfortunately."

She stepped back, flushed. "If you really are busy," she said, "don't change any —"

"I'm not. And Mom said I could have the car for things that were really important."

"It would be okay if you were."

"I know."

"Really."

"I believe you," I said firmly.

"So we'll call each other about Friday? I have to do about a million things with my dad, so just leave a message on the machine."

"I liked finding your book for you."

She grinned at me. "I've got a whole library at home," she said. "Bye."

Gym was the last class of the day, and I hung around afterward watching Tommy Thompson and his friends play a little pickup game of basketball.

I knew most of those guys smoked and drank beer like crazy, but they still looked great. There were a lot of girls standing around talking, leaning toward one another as they whispered, looking out at the polished floor, leaning again, their hair falling together. Boy, sometimes I stand in front of the mirror naked and just hate my body. I don't seem to understand it at all. I feel like I'm the only resident of this big, ugly hotel, but I didn't choose it — somebody checked me in while I was unconscious and now I can't get out.

Anyway, I came out the side door of the gym and there was Sully. "Hey, let's go for a ride or something," he said.

"I thought you always studied right after school."

"I think I need to talk."

"Want to go out to my place?"

"I thought your mom was home until six."

"I mean my land."

He turned to me abruptly. "Want to know what's really bothering me?"

"Sure, I —"

"I think I like Peggy."

"So?"

"I think she likes me."

"The United Nations should have problems like that."

"I was over there the other night listening to music when my folks thought I was at the library, and I asked her if she thought I looked like Sideshow Bob."

"And?"

"She said no."

"So far so good, unless she likes little weird cartoon clowns."

"Walker, it was really nice. I mean, she made something to eat and there was nobody around, but . . ." He left the sentence sticking out like that. "But when I left, she only kissed me on the forehead."

"My aunt does that."

"I know, I know. What do you think it means? Does she like me or not? Or does she just like my forehead?"

"Look," I said, shaking him by the shoulder like he was asleep. "Just relax. Whatever's going to happen will happen. You don't have to do anything."

"Do you really think so? I've read all about this. I even went back and looked up courtship rituals in my dad's anthropology books."

"Just don't bring her a mirror and some beads."

He turned toward me, his face knotted with concern. "You really think there's nothing I should do?"

"Just be yourself. Peggy's always liked you."

"I have to ask somebody. I sure can't ask my dad. All he wants me to do is study." Then he frowned. "Let's get out of here. I can never think in school."

"So this is it?" Sully shaded his eyes like a sea captain. "Did you rip up the ground like that?"

"It's called plowing."

"And then what?"

"Some fertilizer; limestone, I think Mr. Kramer said. Then turn it over again probably, then we plant something and sit back and wait."

"And it grows?"

"That's the idea."

He looked out at the tractor. "And you know how to drive that?"

"Sure."

"Show me."

I fired up the little Farmall, and with Sully holding on to my shoulders we made a round or two.

"This isn't bad," he said as we walked back to the car over the choppy earth.

"Rachel and I sat out here the other day," I told him. "It was really nice."

"You didn't . . . ?"

"No, but we fooled around a little."

"You touched her boobs?"

"No, Doctor."

"God," he said, twirling around in either enthusiasm or frustration. "Look at these hands. All they know how to do is turn the pages of a book. I'll probably be in medical school before I touch a real mammary gland, and then it'll probably be in an operating room. They'll uncover it, and right in front of everybody I'll start salivating. Maybe I should just come right out and ask Peggy if I can touch hers." Then he added hurriedly, "Purely in the interest of science."

"I'll bet that'd be a first even for Peggy."

"Don't rag on Peggy," he snapped.

"I didn't mean —"

He held both hands up, palms out, holdup style. "Sorry, I know you didn't." Then he exhaled, cheeks puffed out like those pictures of the North Wind. "I'm all screwed up, Walker. I used to think I knew everything. All of a sudden it seems like I don't know beans."

Sully was the first sign of trouble, if I'd been paying attention, but I was like a weatherman who feels a few drops, then goes ahead and forecasts fair and warmer.

That night my mom came in late from work. She was crying, and when I went to her room, she looked like she'd just run over Thumper.

"What's —"

She just waved me away and closed the door in my face.

At school the next day, every teacher I had yelled at me for no reason, and worse than that, Rachel didn't show up at all.

Just about the only thing that hadn't gone wrong was working with Mr. Kramer, so of course Friday afternoon the tractor broke down. All I could do was stand around and sweat while he swore and tried to fix it. When I told him that I had a date that night, he said it was just like today's generation to quit when the going got the least bit tough, so like an idiot I decided to prove him wrong, and we didn't finish until nearly eight o'clock.

There was no message from Rachel, and, naturally, no Mom. There wasn't even dinner, just the empty oven ready for any passing suicide. I knew when I dialed that Rachel wouldn't be home, and sure enough, she wasn't. Even the machine was off, probably out with everything else in the world having a good time, everything but me, fanning out a losing hand of frozen dinners, choosing the least obnoxious, taking a shower while it cooked, and looking at my sloping body in the mirror. I was pale except for my arms and the back of my neck. My God, a real redneck. Probably I'd buy a hound dog and start listening to banjo records if I wasn't careful.

The only good thing was that I was so tired I couldn't stay up and worry about Rachel. I went to bed at nine-thirty, and the next thing I knew, my mom was saying that Sully was on the phone.

"I hate to be the one to tell you this," he began, "but Rachel was out with Thompson last night."

"Oh, God. Are you sure?"

"Somebody who's a busboy at the Embers saw them having dinner, and then they went for ice cream."

"Who said?"

"They stopped for gas at the Chevron station; Mark saw them eating sundaes. Hot fudge, I think."

Bradleyville's like Cartoonland: news travels like those wavy lines that drift from house to house while the cartoon characters sleep, and in the morning everybody knows.

"Why don't I come by later," Sully said, "and we'll drown our sorrows."

"I think I ought to talk to Rachel."

"Are you going to be home?"

"Kramer's going to have that piece of mine watered down good and then probably I'll have to turn it over again."

"Well, I'll find you."

"Hello?" Rachel sounded exhausted. Had he kept her out all night? Or worse?

"It's me," I said coldly.

"Walker? How are you?"

"The question is, how are you?"

"Terrible. I've been in bed for two days."

Oh, my God. With Tommy?

"Walker, are you there? When I get my period, I get these terrible cramps."

"Oh," I said, breathing a sigh of relief that would have propelled your average sailboat for hours. "You should have called me."

"I tried, but there was nobody home; anyway, I'm not very good company when I'm like this."

"Didn't you get to go out at all?" Mr. District Attorney strikes again.

"Just once. Dinner with my dad the other night."

"Damn it, Rachel. You went out with Tommy Thompson."

"That's right. My dad and I had dinner with his dad and him."

"Is that all, just dinner?"

"Yes. What's —"

I struck like I'd just caught her in the lie that would alter the course of history. I believe I even said *Aha!* "You had an ice cream with him afterward, just the two of you."

"Were you spying on me?"

"Why, do you have something to hide? Anyway, Bradleyville's a small town. Everybody knows everything about everybody else." I thought of my mom. "Or almost everything."

"Then why don't they know that I almost always go to dinner with my dad when he's doing business?"

"Some business, using his daughter as a —"

"He wants to buy some land from Mr. Thompson, that's all."

"Don't you know what kind of person he is?"

"Mr. Thompson?" she asked.

"No, Tommy. God, he —"

"Of course I know. What do you think girls talk about in the bathroom? The political situation in the Middle East?"

"And you went anyway?"

"Walker, it was just for dinner."

"Don't forget those hot fudge sundaes."

"Oh, well. Bring out the firing squad. That is incriminating."

"I don't want you to go out with him anymore."

There was a long pause, maybe thirty seconds, which seems like an eternity when you're just holding a phone and your hand keeps getting sweatier and sweatier. When she did say something, she sounded really serious.

"We probably shouldn't talk about this right now. You're upset and I still don't feel well. It can't be a good time."

There was another pause, but I could feel something building.

"I've got to say one thing, though, Walker. I don't

want you to tell me who to see or what to do. If I want somebody to run my life, all I have to do is talk to my dad, okay?"

It was my turn to make her wait. I felt terrible, like my chest had turned to stone.

"Walker? Are you there?"

The best I could do was grunt. Lord, if I got any more primitive, I'd go in the kitchen and the pilot light would scare me.

"Okay, then," she said. "I'll say it: let's not see each other for a little while. Now I'm upset, too, and . . . oh, I don't know."

We waited again, and pretty soon I heard the line go dead. I sat down next to the phone on this little milking stool that nobody ever uses. My mother glided by carrying a cup of coffee in one hand and a ten-pound book in the other. I had to hand it to her. She always reads stuff that's hard, never anything with a caped rogue on the cover. She asked if I was okay.

"I guess Rachel and I broke up."

"Honey, I'm sorry."

"Well, maybe we weren't really going together, anyway. It was just kind of an assumption. We'd only been out a couple of times, really, if you don't count the passion by the lockers."

She smiled at me and pointlessly straightened my T-shirt. "You're such a sensible kid," she said. "Such a good, sensible kid. You know when I came in the other night and I'd been crying? There was this guy at the club and we'd had coffee a couple of times and then the next thing I know he's leaving with this twenty-year-old singer who takes off her clothes so fast you'd think she had a rash. I mean, no class at all, just 'Hey, here I am' and 'Hey, look, I'm naked.' Tony hadn't said anything to me; he didn't make any promises. But what do I do when he goes out with Little Miss Fiery Pants? I cry."

It made me nervous to hear about my mother's private life, her other life, the one away from home and me and Dad, or at least his memory. I guess I am a pretty sensible kid. I didn't expect her not to have another life and go out with guys and, I guess, make love and even think about getting married. But I didn't like to hear about it.

As for me, it was pretty clear the kissing had stopped.

As I drove toward the outskirts of town, I put the Rachel conversation on rewind. Boy, parts of it really frosted my balls, especially that stuff about her period.

Girls have all the breaks. They get to wait to be

asked out, they get to say no all the time, and they have their famous periods.

I mean, there are mothers who cry for happiness when their daughters start. It's a regular celebration.

What does a guy do with his first hard-on? It's not like he runs to Dad and they shake hands enthusiastically and Dad hands over a bunch of condoms and says, "Now you're a man, son, because you've got this dandy tool. Treat it carefully. Don't stick it in a sheep or a blender, okay? And gosh darn it, your mother and I are real proud of you."

I was a little late, and the water truck had made a round or two by the time I pulled up. I watched the wide spray sizzle, turn coffee-colored, and trickle into the furrows I'd made.

"Are you all right, son?" asked Mr. Kramer.

"I'm having a little trouble with my girlfriend."

"Why don't you call her and say you're sorry?"

"Sorry for what?" I barked. "I didn't do anything."

"You know best." He looked out across the damp earth.

"Look, is it okay if I pay this guy with a check?"

"No need for that. While ago one of my boys disced that section of Hugo's over by the waterworks."

"I'm sorry I yelled."

"You're just riled about your girlfriend." He touched my shoulder so lightly it was like he was testing wet paint. "Why don't you go on up to the home place and switch that plow there for a single disc. Once we see what that does, we'll sit down and talk about what to do next."

I took off, full-out at twenty-five miles an hour, waving at the other farmers who waited patiently behind me until it was safe to pass and just endured the blaring horns of the city slickers who swept past, their faces as tight as if they'd been rubbed with alum.

All that afternoon I sliced through furrows I'd made just the week before, running more or less perpendicular to them, transforming the easy currents of earth into a stammery chop.

Mr. Kramer was just climbing into his old Chevy when I finished. "This place is so poorly," he said, "the fowl don't even bother. I'd sure like to see a nice fat wren come down here and get himself a bite to eat. Look."

Sure enough, not a quarter mile away the sky was full of punctuation. High above us, dark birds moved in pairs or flocks. If they looked down at my place, they rejected it and I began to feel protective and a little hurt, like having a child so plain he was always chosen last.

Anyway, the birds were probably all over at the Thompsons', with Rachel feeding them off golden plates.

* * *

It was getting late when I saw Sully's big white car come up the frontage road, turn, and park next to mine.

"Sorry I'm late," he said. "I was over at Peggy's."

"Any news about Rachel?"

He shook his head. "Why don't we go out tonight, just two guys on the town."

"I'd probably bump into her and then kill myself. I think I'll just hang around the house."

"You know you're better off without her, don't you?"

"No."

"Who needs a girl like that, anyway?"

"Like what? A girl like what?"

"A girl who lies."

"She didn't lie, exactly. We just had this communication breakdown. I wasn't home when she called."

"If my wife ever lied to me, I'd kill her."

"Great. Some psychiatrist you're going to make. Why don't you just open a gun shop."

"My dad says everybody lies and cheats."

"Oh, screw your dad."

"Hey, watch it."

"You watch it. Whatever happened is between Rachel and me. I don't need your stupid advice, and I sure don't need to hear about your old man."

"Well, at least my father makes a lot of money."

"Compared to mine, you mean, who's busy decomposing for the minimum wage?"

"And at least my mom stays home and doesn't take off her clothes."

"We're all grateful for that."

"She's pretty enough."

"Get serious. She only leaves the house on Halloween."

When Sully gets mad, his freckles sort of light up, and right then he could have stopped cars at a railroad crossing. I thought he might take a swing at me, but instead he whirled on one heel like a drill-team captain and marched back to his car.

Two arguments in one day. Maybe it was in the air, like flu.

When I came slumping into the house, Mom said, "Perk up. We just had a nibble on that property of yours. I was hearing the kind of figures that would send you to college three or four times."

"Oh, God, now I'm going to lose that, too?"

She gave me one of those critical looks mothers are so good at. If she'd been a Geiger counter I'd have crackled like crazy.

"What else have you lost lately?"

"I just had a fight with Sully, and I already told you about Rachel."

"You and Sully have fought before and it's always been okay. What's going on with Rachel, if it's any of my business?"

"It's just this stupid argument. We're both wrong."

"But she's wronger." She looked me up and down like a forester inspecting a stunted tree. "Are you eating enough? You look thinner."

"You may find me tomorrow passed out in the House of Pies."

"That bad?"

"Well, what if I was a little late getting home? That's no reason to start dating the biggest Don Juan in school."

"Are you sure this isn't a little lovers' quarrel that'll work itself out in —"

"And we're not lovers, so don't give me your birth-control speech."

She pushed my hair back in the brusque mother-lion way she has. It's affectionate enough, but about half the time it hurts, too. "I have to go," she said, "but could you maybe not overeat and call Rachel instead? What's the worst that could happen?"

"She could say she couldn't talk now because she was underneath Tommy Thompson."

"I used to feel that way, about your father," she said.

115

"I was really jealous. I'd imagine the craziest things, like he'd go away to a convention for the phone company and meet an ice skater. I guess I thought she'd be whizzing through the corporate offices in her flouncy little skirt. God knows what I thought. And it was always an ice skater or . . ."

I looked up. "What?"

"Nothing."

"C'mon. Either an ice skater or what?"

"A stripper. Do you believe that?"

"Nothing much surprises me today."

I sat in the tub and the soil melted off me. I experimented briefly with my johnson: sure enough, it floated, just like Sully said.

Then I wondered about Rachel. Was she having a good time? With somebody else? Did she realize what a mistake she'd made by going out with me? Would she use her father's powerful connections to put out a contract on me so that no other girl would ever waste her time?

It's funny about jealousy. You never imagine the beloved sleeping and drooling onto her pillow, never sitting on the toilet with an upset stomach, or even just standing around in her underwear and staring into the refrigerator. It's always her laughing gaily and tearing off her blouse in mad abandon while she thinks, *Walker? Walker who?*

As I dried off, I ran down my list of the things I would take into any bomb shelter with me in case of a nuclear attack:

> *Häagen-Dazs blueberry swirl*
> *Reese's peanut butter cups*
> *Ruffles*
> *Trader Joe's almond butter*
> *New York–style cheesecake*

Then I stood in a towel by the phone and thought about calling Rachel. What would I say if I got her? What would she say? Maybe I was afraid she would say she never wanted to speak to me again, ever, and then she'd blow a police whistle in the phone and deafen me for life.

I dialed anyway and got, naturally, that machine. There was her father's big bow-wow voice; there was the beep; there I was not knowing what to say. I sure wasn't going to apologize to a piece of magnetic tape, and who said I was going to apologize at all? I got mad all over again. She could have at least been home, hunched over the phone anxiously. I hung up.

Then I went into my bedroom to get some money and do some serious eating.

* * *

Monday morning was gloomy, with big, swirly, gray clouds off in the west looking like halfhearted erasures on a chalkboard. Even the kids seemed cloudy, drifting through the halls, not saying much.

I took roundabout ways to classes, half afraid I'd run into Rachel. Instead I bumped into Sully.

"I saw her" was the first thing he said.

"Yeah. So?"

"She looked sad."

"Probably lost her new panties in the back of a Trans-Am."

"I don't think Rachel's like that."

I took a deep breath. "I don't either. Look, I'm sorry about the other day."

"Forget it. I told Peggy about what happened and she said I was way out of line. I guess this calls for an apology." He looked up quickly and snapped his finger. "Waiter, bring my friend an apology and be quick about it."

I don't think we knew exactly what to do next. Girls can cry and hug and kiss when they make up. If we'd tried that, they'd have our parents on the phone and us down at the school nurse for sedation.

"How's Peggy?"

"Peggy's okay. I'm taking your advice. *Que sera sera,* right?"

"So Rachel looks sad, huh?"

118

"Uh-huh. I thought about you last night. Was it Pig City?"

"That was the plan. Instead I lay down on my bed for a minute just to get up enough strength to call Pizza Man, He Delivers, and the next thing I knew it was one-thirty and everything was closed."

"Will you be around later?"

"Yeah, or out at the Land Time Forgot."

"Maybe I'll see you, except . . ."

"You might go over to Peggy's?"

"Yeah. Peggy says you ought to talk to Rachel." He held up an index finger like a teacher shushing a class. "Even if it was Rachel's fault. She says the guy —"

"So Peggy says, huh? What does Peggy say about what your father says?" I wasn't being mean; Sully and I were just tossing the ball back and forth.

"Well, Peggy says that what my father says is mostly bullshit."

"And I say she's right. Look, I gotta go." My English teacher was holding the door open for me; he was sort of bowing from the waist and inviting me in with his free hand. Very droll.

"Look," Sully said, backing away and talking fast like someone reasoning with a mad bomber, "you'll bump into her and it'll be fine."

But it wasn't fine. I not only didn't bump into her; I

119

didn't even see her, not for four days. I admit that on Tuesday I took some roundabout paths to a class or two myself, mostly because I still wasn't sure what I'd say to Rachel if I did see her, and I was kind of afraid of what she'd say to me; but on Wednesday and Thursday I started loitering seriously, propped up supercasually all over the place. But still no Rachel.

To my great relief I saw Tommy Thompson, and to my even greater relief he was with Sheila Webster, who was hanging all over him. But no Rachel.

I dragged myself to work every afternoon, and it was on Friday that I looked up from fiddling with the carburetor on the tractor to see Sully's dad's Cadillac glide down the frontage road and slip in beside my mom's old Saturn. Peggy got out and waved, then Sully, and then right out of the back seat came Rachel, wearing a blue sundress with a huge white daisy on the skirt and two more on top. I walked toward them slowly, watching my step on the uneven ground; I sure didn't want to blow this reconciliation by tripping and falling on my face.

"Hi, you guys," I said. I'd taken off the leather gloves Mr. Kramer had lent me and I waved one. Then I said self-consciously, "I'll get my shirt, it's over —"

"That's okay," said Rachel.

Could I have forgotten how soft her voice was?

"Rachel," Sully said formally, "this is Walker Davis.

He doesn't own a shirt, but otherwise he's a nice guy. And Walker, I'd like you to meet Rachel Gardner. Rachel just transferred from New York and has never seen dirt before, so I thought we'd bring her by your place here because you've got tons of it."

"Yeah, well. This is it, all right." I made a sweeping ringmaster's gesture.

"It's looking better," said Rachel. "Sitting up and taking nourishment."

"Sully," Peggy said. "I think these two might want to talk privately."

They ambled away, both pointing elaborately. I put my hands in my pockets. Rachel linked hers in front like a little kid in church. Then we looked at each other again.

"I'm really sorry," I said.

"God, me too. Really."

"It was all my fault," I said.

"No, it was all my fault."

"Honestly, Rachel, it was me."

"Okay, you win. It was all your fault."

"Huh?"

She had this enormous smile and her teeth were whiter than the daisies on her dress. "Just a little humor," she said, "to lighten the situation." She reached for my right arm, taking hold of it with both hands like she was going to shake a kite out of a tree, then sliding down until both her hands held one of mine. "We were both wrong," she said. "You shouldn't have been late; I should have called from the restaurant. . . ."

We tugged at each other, both stepping forward at the same time. We stood, swaying, just inches apart. I couldn't believe how good she smelled. We both licked our lips slowly, two cats who got the cream.

"I hate people who can't settle their differences," said Sully, coming up behind us.

"Shut up," Peggy said mildly. "You spoiled it."

"Are you guys okay?" I said, turning away reluctantly.

"Fine," they said in unison.

"Nice place you've got here." Peggy was wearing green pedal pushers, a man's green shirt tied at the waist, and a green hat with a veil. She looked like every string bean's idea of beauty. "It makes a girl want to get down there in the dirt and grow things."

"If you're serious," I said, "Mr. Kramer and I are planting tomorrow. You could help."

"Me too?" said Sully.

"Everybody, sure. Just be here at six," I said.

"Not in the morning."

I nodded.

We began to drift toward the cars. Rachel put her arm around me and I was acutely conscious of her fingers tucked inside my waistband.

We waited awkwardly beside Sully's father's belligerently shiny Cadillac.

"Uh, why don't you guys stick around?" Rachel said lamely.

"Yeah," I muttered. "Stick around."

"We should stay," Peggy said. "Just to drive them crazy."

We wanted to be alone, but once we were, neither of us knew exactly what to do. I looked toward the car, then decided against it — too crude. But she was looking, too.

"Do you need to get home?" I asked.

"No. I was just . . . thinking."

"About my mom's Saturn?"

"Sort of."

"You look good, Rachel."

"You too."

"I'm just dirty in a couple of the right places; you're pretty."

"Peggy came over the other day and we went through my stuff. She showed me what to wear with what, and she was right. She breaks all those stupid fashion rules and she's still right."

"Did she pick this out?" I felt the hem of her dress. Even it was warm.

Rachel shook her head. "I did. But I was thinking of you all the time."

I took her hand. The sun was setting and the back window of the car glowed like neon: VACANCY.

"What'd your dad think of Peggy?"

"He'd like it if I had a hundred girlfriends and no boyfriends at all."

"He doesn't like me?"

"It's not you exactly. He's just used to getting my undivided attention."

Rachel stopped and leaned against one dented fender. I kicked the tires lightly like a timid shopper.

"You didn't have boyfriends before?"

"I was a lot younger," she said sensibly. "And he didn't want me to really like some guy and then have to move away."

"Your dad said that?"

"We talk really easily. And he was probably right. But things are different now. I'm not fourteen and we're not going to move. And even if we were, I'd like you anyway."

Her eyes — blue this time to match the dress she had picked out all by herself — met mine and held.

"So do you want to sit in the car a little while before we go?" I asked.

"God, yes."

I don't think the doors had even slammed before Rachel and I started kissing like there was no tomorrow. I kissed her shoulders and arms. I kissed her neck and ears and I even did this weird thing by mistake where I had my tongue in her nose for a second.

I even kissed the straps on her sundress, nibbling up and down them like a man eating corn. Rachel unbuttoned the shirt I had just buttoned and put her hand inside, which about drove me crazy; and then she started to make these random passes at my crotch. Or at least I think that was what was happening. So I peeked, and there was her right arm roaming around in the air like somebody trying to find a shoe under the bed. One minute it would be really close and the next way out over the floorboards. I felt like playing that kids' game where you shout, "Cold, cold, warmer, warmer, hot, hot, hot!"

Rachel and I were holding on to one another, still kissing, naturally, but also taking a little break, when she said, "Don't forget your mother."

I couldn't believe it. I'd just been thinking about my mom and what she'd said about birth control, because for the first time in my life it was clear to me that I might actually need it.

I sat up and buttoned my shirt while Rachel shook out her skirt with both hands like someone making a bed.

"Walker, have you ever done this before? What we just did, I mean the kissing and the other?"

"The other?"

She looked down at her hands. "You know, how we touched?"

I wondered what she wanted to hear. Would a yes hurt her feelings, making her seem than less special? Would a no make me a wimp?

"Not really," I lied, "but . . ."

"I guess I'm interested in how I did." She sounded like a scholarship student. "Peggy," she continued, "gave me a few hints." Her eyes widened. "Some I'll have to save until I'm thirty-five."

"It all felt great. Honest."

"I got dizzy," she said happily.

"Me too."

"I wish we didn't have to go."

"I wish we could just stay here until they built the mall over us."

"That stupid mall," she said mildly. "I like this place just the way it is."

As we drove, Rachel put her arm around my shoulders and played with my hair. I was really flattered. No one had ever done anything like that, but I'd seen it a thousand times with guys older than me or better-looking or with hotter cars. I could have driven around like that forever, Bradleyville's version of the Flying Dutchman.

I made a left at Octavia, going a block or two out of

my way in hopes a few more people would see me being so eagerly caressed.

"Your grades are pretty good, aren't they?" she asked.

Perfect: a carful of guys passed, going the other way. "Huh? Oh, yeah, I guess."

She trailed her fingers across the back of my neck. "Do you ever feel insecure?"

"Only in the daytime and at night. Otherwise I'm fine."

Rachel smiled and kissed my shoulder, light as a wand.

"Mr. Jenkins, my physics teacher, told me I didn't belong in his accelerated class," she said. "He told me he thought my counselor had made a mistake."

"Jenkins is that way. It's his idea of motivation. He tried it on Sully."

"Did he on you?"

"I don't take those high-powered classes. Since I don't know where I'm going, I guess I'm in no real hurry to get there."

"God, I used to be smart." She stroked my neck, giving me long, smooth pets like I was a llama. "Mr. Jenkins really made me wonder."

I guess we're all pretty much the same down deep. I mean, Rachel seemed to have it made — she was cute and had great clothes; she was rich; she'd been to interesting places and met important people. Yet she lay awake and wondered, too. All over town kids lay awake and wondered: Am I smart enough, pretty enough, strong enough, tall enough? If our fears were smoke, the town would be covered night and day by an inky pall.

"Walker, do you think I'm smart?"

I hesitated again, wondering what she wanted to hear and pretty much knowing what that was. Instead, though, I said, "I don't know, Rachel." I turned to her, letting the car drive itself for a few seconds. "I'm sure you are, but I've only really known you for a little while, so . . ."

I thought for a second she might cry, and I was afraid I'd done the wrong thing by trying to do the right one. Instead, she kissed me.

"What a great answer," she exclaimed. "God, any other guy would've said, 'Yeah, sure, of course,' just to be nice or to make me feel better or whatever. Instead, you just told the truth." She put both arms around me and squeezed. "Oh, Walker, let's always tell each other the truth, okay? Always."

That was my chance to turn to her and say, "Look, about my mom . . ." But the words wouldn't come out. I opened my mouth and nothing happened.

It was still dark when I left the house the next morning, but when I got to Rachel's, her father was already on the telephone, probably buying all the land south of the equator. He waved me into a seat, his manicured hand lolling in the sleeve of a velour robe. Nothing had been unpacked yet. Crates were still stacked around the spacious rooms; a suitcase lined in pink stood open, looking like an alligator that ate linen.

"Good Christ," he said, hanging up the phone. "They act like I'm asking them to rezone the world."

"Who's that?" I asked politely.

"The city council."

"Is this for the Garden of Gardner?"

He brightened. "Rachel told you. What about it? Tell me what you think."

"I don't know exactly. It seems . . ."

"Do you like Westgate?"

"The old mall? No, I . . ."

"Good for you. Westgate's everything a mall doesn't have to be. It's overscaled and it's dull. People only go there because it's more fun than downtown."

"There isn't much downtown to go to, thanks to Westgate."

"You think the mall pulled people out of the city? I think Bradleyville drove people to the mall. There's always something to look at in a mall, always something to touch. And it's all free and it's all safe."

"I thought you just said it was dull."

"Compared to the Garden it is. Compared to the

Garden it's like an old stripper who never takes off her clothes. Who cares anyway, right?"

"I care, that's who."

"About what?"

"Uh . . . malls."

He was getting excited, and poured himself some coffee from a silver carafe.

"Really? Have you ever been to Milan?" He didn't wait for an answer. "That's where old Giuseppe Mengoni started it all in 1865, and it's still great: it's the original hundred-percent location."

I wondered what Rachel was doing upstairs, but I dutifully asked, "What's a hundred-percent location?"

"A place that everybody has to pass and there's something going on twenty-four hours a day."

"Sounds good if you have the pay-toilet concession."

He frowned, but not at my silly joke. "That's what I want for Bradleyville. We're living in the center of the United States." He tapped on the table with his blunt but manicured index finger. "This could be the one-hundred-percent location for the republic."

"I'm almost ready," Rachel shouted from somewhere above us.

"Are you being nice to my daughter?" he asked abruptly.

"Or do I just hit her with the hose in places where it won't show?"

He snorted instead of laughed. "I apologize. It's just that Rachel has never been mistreated for an instant by anyone anywhere. I know you're good to her. She likes you. She told me so herself."

"I like her, too."

"What about Kramer?"

"I don't like him as much, but then we haven't been dating as long."

He smiled that patented half smile. "Irreverent," he said, "but not abrasive." And he looked at me like I was one of my mother's expensive wines. "And you know how to cut through the crap. I like that. I might be able to use you, Walker."

I didn't know what to say. Was he offering me a job? If so, doing what? Cutting through the crap?

"I talked to your mother and I talked to Kramer. She said to ask you."

"What about?"

"Talking to Kramer."

I shrugged. "Talk to him about . . ."

"Selling. Selling your land. Both of you. Or at least giving me an option to buy."

"I thought he wanted to sell."

"I thought he did, too. Now I'm hearing a lot of b.s. about the old homestead."

Just then Rachel came downstairs, sleepy and cute in low boots and jeans.

"Be careful," said her father, a comment that had as many layers as a wedding cake.

Outside of town, Sully and Peggy sat on the hood of the Cadillac and waited; four Styrofoam cups of coffee steamed by the hood ornament, and Rachel reached for one with both hands.

"I must be nuts," she said, smiling. "Where's the sun?" Then to Peggy, "You look great, kid."

"You like it?" She flounced the wide skirts of her prom dress. Or rather she flounced half her prom dress.

"The Cub Scout shirt is a nice touch," said Sully. He pointed to the sleeve. "This poor little weenie only got one stripe and that was for deportment. I can just see him sitting in the corner being good."

"I only got two," I said. "One for deportment and the other for starting fires."

"They gave a stripe for arson?" asked Peggy.

"Campfires."

Peggy rolled the sleeves of her shirt up to reveal a single pink opera glove. Then she tied the shirttails at her navel, revealing an inch or two of the whitest skin I'd ever seen.

"Let's go to work," she said, rubbing her hands together. "Let's plant them seeds, get in the crop, and get rich."

I pointed. "Here comes Mr. Kramer now," and we watched his truck negotiate the dirt road, then stop and shudder as he got out. Mr. Kramer motioned for us, then patted the hood consolingly as the old Chevy quaked one last time, then settled down with a hiss.

I introduced my friends. If he thought twice about somebody in half a dress, it didn't show; he calmly shook Peggy's gloved hand, then touched his cap politely.

"I saw Rachel last night," he said. "Her father poured so much wine in me I felt like a tough piece of meat he was trying to marinate." Then he turned to me. "I tried to get hold of you the other day and got your momma instead."

"I was probably in school. Did you want . . ."

"Nice woman, your mother. Said to talk to you. Said the land was yours and you were grown-up enough to do the right thing. Even apologized for being in bed at ten o'clock in the morning. Said she was a dancer and it was hard work. Made me wonder afterward if I might have seen her on the TV."

"A dancer?" said Rachel. "I thought —"

"Bartender mostly," Peggy said quickly. "But she can dance if . . ." She looked at me helplessly.

"I thought she was a waitress."

"Well," I said, "she's a bartender-waitress."

Then, since I had the hyphens out anyway, I didn't see any harm in using one more. "Actually a bartender-waitress-dancer in this little club, uh, bar-restaurant . . ."

"In Kansas City," Sully said. "We went once, remember, to pick her up after work?"

"Oh, yeah. And it was nice: quiet, clean, a really nice neighborhood. And she doesn't have to dance much, just when things get slow."

"Or really busy," said Sully when Rachel looked bewildered.

"How weird," she said, shaking her head.

"What'd you call me about?" I asked Mr. Kramer, desperate for any diversion.

"Oh, about this place. I just wondered if you were dead set on selling."

"Aren't you?"

He shook his head slowly. "DiPrima neither, and none of the Fiscus boys. It's not just us bumpkins, either. People in Bradleyville ain't so sure anymore. Little by little not everybody's sold on their hometown being the hub of the universe."

I guess we all turned to look at Rachel. She just

grinned and said sensibly, "Well, we can't settle it this morning. Anyway, it's Daddy's problem. Why don't we do what we came for and get to work on this place?"

"Here's all there is to it," Mr. Kramer said, motioning for Sully and me to lift four or five sacks of grain out of the scarred truck bed. He handed each of us a wide sling. "This here goes over one shoulder," he said. "The seeds go into the bottom, then you walk along and scatter it like you're feeding chickens."

"With our hands?" asked Peggy, looking at her indigo nails.

"Yes, ma'am."

"Everybody does it this way?"

"No, ma'am. Nobody does it this way. There's machines could seed this section here before noon, but this is how we used to do it and just about the only way four people can be part of things."

"I'm ready," said Rachel, holding open her scratchy burlap. "Fill 'er up."

A few minutes later, Mr. Kramer told us to spread out. We made a ragged line, throwing seeds every which way. Down on one end, Mr. Kramer walked as easily as a sailor, his right arm moving as smoothly as any MC's introducing star after star. Peggy, beside him, picked up the rhythm first, then Sully, Rachel, and me. We began to work more or less together and the grain went out from us, long scallops in the air, falling without a sound.

It was pretty in a way; Mr. Kramer so smooth and professional; Peggy grinning, her skirt rocking like a bell in a gale; Rachel intent, biting her lower lip, trying to do it right; Sully and me horsing around, throwing handfuls of seed at each other, then pretending to be blinded.

"Look!" Rachel shouted, pointing behind her like someone in a sci-fi movie who has just spotted the nine-foot grasshoppers. We whirled to see — birds. They were having breakfast at our expense.

"What do we do?"

"Nuke 'em," said Sully.

"Send out for cats," Peggy suggested.

"I'd say drop a little extra seed." I glanced at Mr. Kramer, who had just gone on without us, his hand passing through the air in front of him almost jauntily, like someone coming in the door and sailing his hat toward the couch.

We worked that way all morning, and it was hard. At half past ten or so, Peggy staggered over to Rachel and presently they announced they were going to buy lunch for us all. Sully hung in a little longer, then dropped out as we turned again near the cars. Mr. Kramer and I closed ranks and kept up the pace. It was hypnotic in a way: the scrunch of grain in my bare hand, the cool, clean feel of it in my palm where everything else was hot and gritty, the whoosh of the throw, the look of it in the sun flashing like rice at a wedding party.

Every time I worked out there, driving the tractor, cutting back grass along the fence row, hoeing at the weeds that seemed to come up overnight, I just didn't think — not about school, not about the future, not about my mom. Working, I thought just about what I was doing. Or even better, I thought about nothing, my mind as clean and white as the plate I set out for my dinner at night.

Still, I was glad to see Peggy and Rachel come back. And I may as well admit it: I expected Mr. Kramer to pat me on the back and say what a good job I'd done. Instead, he just took the sling off my shoulder and threw it in the back of the truck.

"Are we finished?" I asked.

"For today. Anyway, I am." If he didn't praise me, he didn't criticize, either. I guess he figured people did their best and that was that.

He ambled over to where everybody was sitting, politely took off his battered old hat, and said to Rachel, without any irony, "You can tell your daddy I'm thinking on his generous offer."

"We brought plenty," she said. "Eat with us."

"I think I'll just go on home and lie down."

We watched him walk to his car; then we all waved.

"It must be funny to be alone," Rachel said.

"Boy," said Peggy. "My mom left me alone. I mean they probably cut the cord, she jumped off the table, and off she went to the mall for a new red dress. And speaking of shopping for a red dress, I don't think it'd be so bad to have another mall."

Rachel agreed, suddenly so dreamy it was like she'd heard the magic word. "They're special places." Then she quoted her father, source of all mall wisdom. "They've got their own rules and their own reality."

"What happens to all this?" I took a huge bite of the last sandwich, one that had slipped off the blanket. I didn't bother to wipe off the dirt, though. I'd show them: I liked land so much I would eat it.

"Walker, that's progress."

"Yeah? That's some term for a steady decline."

"I get along okay in malls," Peggy said. "I just sort of zone out and spend."

"You're the Captivated Shopper," Rachel explained, "a Star in the Retail Drama."

I could hear those capital letters and it got on my nerves.

"And that's good?"

Rachel began to get defensive. "Everything there is upbeat. Can that be bad? People have enough crime and

138

stuff in the real world. They don't want to go downtown and look at the empty buildings. At the mall they don't have to think about things like that. The weather is always the same; they can afford to talk to a stranger; and they don't ever have to be afraid of getting ripped off. Tenants have to be honest or they'll get kicked out of the mall. It's in their lease."

"That's just the point. I don't want people to have to be honest because it's in their lease. I just want them to be honest, period."

"People in the mall care, and not just because they have to."

"No, they don't. They care as long as people are lined up at the cash register."

Sully and Peggy followed all this like tennis fans, their heads whipping back and forth at each exchange.

"Well, they're merchants, Walker, not missionaries."

"They aren't even merchants. Just ask somebody in a mall to wait while you go home and get the wallet you forgot, or even better, promise you'll pay him tomorrow. He'll laugh in your face."

"That's no way to run a business."

"Yeah, well, my dad used to forget his wallet all the time. I'd ride back down on my bike with the money."

"Actually," said Sully, "a mall is like a giant womb, so in a way shopping is like a mass return to the —"

But I wasn't finished. "And as for your father saving anything, like he claimed this morning, grow up. He just wants to be king. He makes up a kingdom, modestly calls it the Garden of Gardner, eats up a little town in the process, but what the —"

"He's not a king!" Rachel pounded her knees in frustration. "And he's not bad. He's good. He is."

No one knew exactly what to do then. We all stared off in different directions like lost travelers.

Finally Peggy said brightly, "So, I guess this means shopping is out of the question."

"This is perfect," said Sully, watching the two girls stroll away. "You argued, you laughed at yourselves, you apologized."

"So?"

"So Rachel really likes you. I think she wants you, pardner. She wants your little buns."

"Well, she can't have them. All my pants would fit funny."

"You know, Rachel looks better these days."

"She said Peggy went through her closet with her."

"Not just her clothes."

"Peggy cut her hair, too."

He waved away my simple facts. "Not just that stuff.

She looks more together somehow. Maybe I was just wrong about her. I mean, she's too blocky for me, but —"

"Blocky?"

He drew a rectangle in the air. "Blocky. From the shoulders right down to the hips."

"I really beg your pardon. Rachel's got a waist."

"Have you seen it?"

"I know it's there."

"Well, she's a thousand times better than Debbie. You were never going to get anywhere with Debbie. She was just this Blarney Stone."

"Come again?"

"Something that sat there while you kissed it and wished. But Rachel . . ." He raised his eyebrows lecherously. "You'll tell me when you do it, won't you?"

"I'll hop right up and run to the nearest pay phone. Girls like that, anyway, so Rachel won't mind."

Sully shoved me playfully and I toppled over. Above me was the sky, calmly turning red and orange for the zillionth time. Had the sky ever been young?

Rachel and I watched the car disappear up the unpaved road that ran parallel to the two-lane blacktop. We stood there and waved almost till the taillights disappeared. Then I turned to her uneasily.

"I know I already said I was sorry, but I guess I want to say it again. I don't know what got into me. I didn't mean your dad wanted to be king. I don't even know your dad very well."

"It's okay. I'm sorry, too. I hate myself when I talk like that. I sound like a salesperson. And as far as my dad goes, he probably does want to be king. Just because I'm so protective of him doesn't mean he isn't a real pain sometimes."

I glanced around me: forty acres of recently seeded soil — the earth dark and rich as chocolate — and the rind of the sun glowing at the edge of the world.

"I'm just really attached to this place, I guess."

"Who wouldn't be? I don't think I want to see this covered up any more than you do."

"It is kind of a shame, but like you said, it's progress. Not just for your dad to build a kingdom, but for me to go to college."

She nodded thoughtfully. Then without saying anything we walked — my arm around her shoulders, hers around my waist — toward the nearest property line.

"Do you think they're growing already?" said Rachel, squatting down to get a closer look.

"Germinating maybe. Getting ready. Mr. Kramer says they'll be up before we know it. It's so great how the seeds just wait and wait. Then one day they get covered up, and bingo."

We made our way to the car, with Rachel looking over her shoulder every now and then just to make sure she wasn't missing anything.

Politely I opened the door on her side, then settled in beside her. She smiled the sweetest, warmest smile and put her arms around me.

We didn't even fumble all over the place; our clothes, or part of them, anyway, just receded like the tide.

I'd never seen Rachel's skin before, and it was beautiful.

When I finally touched her, it was so completely mysterious, like nothing else I'd ever felt in my life. It was wonderful, even though it was awkward in the car, lying down like that with my forehead on the torn arm rest and the weird smell of a car's nooks and crannies. I could see down into the crack between the seats, and as odd a time as it was for an inventory, I remember every little thing: a Beeman's gum wrapper, a dime, a Bic pen, a button, hair, a cigarette. A cigarette? Who smoked?

"It's okay," she said. "Walker, it's okay."

Rachel and I sat up. We must have looked like profiles in a shooting gallery.

"Things kind of took me by surprise," I said.

"It's pretty messy, isn't it?"

"They never covered that part in health ed."

"You look kind of disappointed."

The truth was, I was thinking there really wasn't that much to tell Sully. Some great lover I turned out to be. But I said, "I'm only disappointed in myself."

"Don't be. You were so nice, and it felt good. Honest."

"For as long as it lasted."

"Did it hurt you?" she asked.

"God, no. How about you?"

"At first, and then no."

"I guess we should get something so you won't get pregnant."

She got this really wary look on her face.

"Things. For birth control."

"Could I get pregnant from this?"

"I really doubt it. I mean, I've heard of sperms swimming for miles but I've never heard of them hiking over upholstery first."

Rachel put her arms around me again. She smelled so good. God, we'd been working all day and then we'd fooled around and she still smelled wonderful. She smelled like us.

That night I lay in bed half waiting for the sound of my mother's car in the driveway. I had my hands behind my head and I imagined myself shot from above by a sensitive movie director. Did I look different? What would the film record? Insomniac? Pensive teen? Complacent stud? Former jerk-off artist?

So now I was a man. Was my diploma in the mail? And how about my lost innocence — where did it go? Would I stumble on it someday at the car wash, hold it up fondly, and remember this girl named Rachel? Or would we still be together? Was that even possible?

I tried to analyze what it felt like not to be a virgin anymore. I had stepped away from the millions who were and joined the millions who weren't.

Glancing at the clock, I smoothed my superhero bedspread. Batman had a thing for Catwoman, so we knew what side of the line he was on. How about the Lone Ranger? Was he that lone? Or was there someone he could go home to and gratefully take off his mask and boots? Tonto, maybe?

The next thing I knew it was two-thirty and something was wrong. Slowly I reached for my Louisville Slugger; slowly I made my way down the hall. Then, there it was — Mom's bedroom and the immaculate bed, bigger than I'd ever seen it. And emptier.

I knew I couldn't call Sully; his folks would go crazy. Mr. Gardner wouldn't understand. And anyway, what would I say? That I'd lost my mother?

Quickly I checked all the places where we usually

left notes for each other. She couldn't have committed suicide; she liked her horrible job too much. Could she have just abandoned me? Did she know about that afternoon?

> *Dear Walker,*
> *Now that you are a man, I am free at last.*
> *I plan to strip my way around the world.*
> *Don't forget to wear a hat when it's cold.*
>
> > *Cordially,*
> > *Virginia (Mom)*

If she'd had an accident, wouldn't the police call? What if she was stranded somewhere in that stupid old car with 129,000 miles on it? What if she'd gone out with someone from the club and he turned out to be a maniac?

I started to dial the police, then hung up. Probably there was a completely rational explanation. Probably she'd just had to work overtime. Probably the whole menagerie was sick again, not to mention the band and the bouncer.

But why hadn't she called? Why hadn't she at least called? Wasn't I worth one rollover minute?

It was four-thirty when I heard the car coast into the garage. I was woozy with anxiety and calories. I'd finished a two-hour binge by trying to defrost a frozen pie with hot water. Finally I just gave up and ate; it tasted like a plate with apples painted on it.

"I guess," she said, spotting me at the table, "that I hoped you'd be asleep."

"Where were you?" My throat was frozen from the pie and I could feel the cold words.

"Out with a guy." She put her bag down on the sink and looked in the refrigerator. "Pretty bare in here. I feel like Old Mother Hubbard."

"I'll bet Mother Hubbard never stayed out all night."

"Probably not," she said with a small sigh. Then she turned to me. "I'm sorry, sweetheart."

"I was worried." I was also determined not to cry.

She patted my shoulder, then rubbed it and frowned like she'd found a dirty word written there. "I know."

"I thought you were dead."

"I should have called. I meant to, and then it was midnight and I didn't want to wake you. I called Millie."

"Next door?"

"She never goes to bed before twelve. She said everything looked peaceful and quiet over here."

"I woke up a couple of hours ago. God, Mom. I didn't know what to think." I could feel my face scrunching up; some man I'd just become.

She leaned and put her cool cheek against my forehead.

"I know, honey. If I do it again, I'll call you. Earlier. Every hour on the hour if you want."

I reached for the lapels of her red jacket and hung on.

"Are you going to do it again?"

"I might. I don't know. But not like this, I promise."

She leaned to kiss me. She smelled like the outdoors, like night. "Are you mad?"

I shook my head. "Not much, not anymore."

"I need a glass of wine. Will you sit with me? I don't want to be alone right now."

I nodded, not letting go of her, though.

She moved the carton with MOM'S PIES written on it. As she poured a glass of red wine she asked, "What'd you do, suck a frozen pie?"

"Something like that."

"Lord, Walker." She sounded more amazed than miffed. Then I felt her appraise me. "Do you want some wine? We could have a drink together. First time for everything, as they say."

"I don't know about pie and chili and cookies and wine."

"I see your point." She sat down with a whoosh. "Can I put my feet on your knees?" She looked around curiously. "You didn't eat the other chair, did you?"

"I was standing on it in the pantry." I turned and made room on my lap.

Mom tasted her zinfandel, put her head back so the wine could trickle down her throat, and whispered, "Ah." Then she said to me, "This guy that I was out with?"

"Uh-huh."

"He had a wooden foot."

"How do you know that?"

"When we were fooling around, it fell off."

"God."

"He'd told me before. We were being frank, I guess. I was talking about your dad and you."

"So he brought up his wooden foot?"

"Something like that. There was a mine in Vietnam, V.A. hospital, that kind of stuff. Then we were at his place on the couch and, you know, the music's playing and everything's fine and boom, his foot falls off." She wrinkled her nose. "Not too romantic."

I couldn't help but smile. "No kidding." I couldn't help but think of Rachel, either. What had happened that afternoon hadn't been completely romantic either. Just premature.

"Anyway, that's when I knew it was time to go home, when parts of their bodies start falling off."

"So did you?"

"Go home? Yes, sort of. It took a little while."

"What'd he want to do, walk you to your car?"

My mom started to laugh, holding her wine out in front

of her so it wouldn't spill, looking at me, laughing harder, leaning forward, then finally standing up and all the time lifting her glass higher and higher in a kind of toast.

"God," she said, wiping her eyes with a kitchen towel, "your dad could make me laugh like that."

"Do you ever miss him?" I asked.

"Honey, tonight I miss him so much it hurts clear through to my spine." She took a tiny sip of wine. "And not just because his feet didn't fall off in bed, either."

"But you two were really different. You said so: he wanted this, you wanted that."

"That doesn't mean I didn't love him. You guys were different, too, Walker. But you loved him."

"I never told him."

"It would have scared him to death. We'd have had to leave his dinner out on the porch for a week."

"Do you think he knew?"

"Yes," she said firmly. "Like I know that —"

I interrupted. "That he loved you?"

She smiled hugely. "That you love me."

I nodded, all choked up. God, what a day: intercourse, carbohydrate overload, tearful confessions.

"And," she added, "disapprove of me."

I raised my empty hands helplessly.

She took one, clasping it. "It's all right. You told the

truth and the world didn't collapse. Besides, I'm not nuts about you all the time, either."

"You're not?" I said, sniffling and only half kidding. "Would you like me more if I ate less?"

"No, and I wouldn't like you less if you ate more."

"Seriously?"

"Seriously. But Rachel might feel differently."

"I know. It couldn't be much fun to only get your arms halfway around somebody. It's too much like measuring a sequoia."

"Are you two doing all right?"

"She's really nice, Mom."

"She seems nice."

I thought for a second I might tell her what had happened that afternoon. Then I didn't. It didn't seem like the considerate thing to do. I was afraid she would worry about me, not because she didn't trust me, but — it finally dawned on me — because she loved me.

The next day Sully was waiting for me outside my English class.

"How was it after Peggy and I left? Did you guys fight again, or what?"

I shook my head. "Just the opposite."

"The opposite opposite?"

"Uh-huh."

His eyes got brighter. "You're kidding. What was it like?"

"Better than ice cream" I said.

"Oh, my God."

People in the halls turned to stare. It did sound like he was having a religious experience.

"And," I added, "it lasted about twenty seconds."

His voice dropped to a whisper. "What happened?"

"I happened."

"Oh." Sully thought for a second. "So what? It was your first time. What did Rachel say?"

"That it was messy." I filled in the details. "But that it felt good."

"She was a virgin?"

"I think so."

"Do you want some advice?"

"No."

"Do it again as soon as possible."

"Sully, I didn't just fall off a horse."

"It's the same thing. It's all pattern-making and behavior modification."

"Do you really think I should?"

"Don't you want to?"

"Sure, but how?"

"At your house."

"Are you nuts?"

"It's perfect. Your mom's always gone. Tell Rachel you want to study together."

"Why not just tell her the truth?"

He shook his head. "Too risky. Just get her over there first. Then make love for about an hour."

"Hold it. Let me get this straight: I call her and say, 'Come over and study.' Then instead I make love to her for an hour. Isn't she going to suspect something when she comes in with her books and there I stand with a clock and a hard-on?"

"Just call. She wants to do it as much as you do."

"Really?"

"Girls are mammals just like boys."

"Oh, okay. Right after she gets in the door, I'll just say, 'Baby, you're a mammal just like me,' then she'll moan and tear off her clothes."

Sully looked down at the floor. "I sound like a jerk sometimes, don't I?"

I put my hand on his bony shoulder. "No. I mean yes, but no."

"You should be the one giving me advice. I'm the virgin, not you. Some psychiatrist I'm going to make. My clients will say, 'Doctor, sex bothers me a lot.' And I'll say, 'Sex? What's that?'"

"No, you won't."

"Do you know why I don't try to make love with Peggy?" he asked abruptly. "Because I'm afraid she'll laugh at me. I like Peggy and she likes me, but I'm so scared she'll compare me to some superstud she's known that . . ."

"I don't think Peggy would ever do that."

"Honestly?" He dropped his doctor act completely. He really wanted to know.

"Honestly. Besides, when you whisper that you're both mammals, how can she resist?"

"What's Sully laughing about?" asked Rachel, waving to him as he retreated.

"Boy talk," I said facetiously.

"Not about me, I hope."

"Oh, Rachel, no. Really."

She took my hand quickly. "I know. I'm sorry." She looked down, then up, down again, and up like someone consulting a guidebook, matching the picture with the site.

"Do you feel different?" she asked quietly.

"Not really, do you?"

She shook her head. "I even inspected myself in the mirror."

"You look the same, but you always look good to me."

She moved closer. "You always look good to me, too."

The warning bell rang. "Why, uh, why don't we, uh, study together tonight?"

"Okay. My house?"

"No, uh . . . over there." I pointed toward home, but I couldn't seem to get the words out.

She looked puzzled. "Over where?"

"You know."

"What, the library?"

"Mine," I croaked.

"Yours?"

"My house," I gasped.

"What about your mom?"

"She'll be gone. We won't bother anybody. We can get a lot done." Oh, I felt slimy. But Rachel had this shy little smile.

"Okay," she said. "What time?"

I couldn't believe my ears. Then she was gone to class, and I was alone in the hall trying to arrange my books casually in front of me so that nobody could see. Either that, or I could claim *Silas Marner* was the most stimulating novel I'd ever read, and I could prove it.

That afternoon Sully and I were loading my old Schwinn into the back of the Cadillac when he stopped and asked, "Why did you take this thing today? When I came by and your mom said you'd ridden your bike to school, I couldn't believe it."

"You're a teen psychiatrist — you tell me."

"Maybe just a little trip down Memory Lane? You took a big step yesterday; you said goodbye to your childhood." Idly he spun the front wheel. "God, remember how we used to clip playing cards on these? What was all that about, anyway?"

"Are you kidding? It made the bicycles sound like cars. That's all we talked about, owning a car and having girlfriends. Which reminds me, let's get this show on the road."

We settled into the red leather seats. Not far away sat Rachel's little Firebird.

"So," said Sully, "where to?"

"Your friendly neighborhood prophylactic emporium."

"Aha. Well, thank God they don't come in sizes. Remember when we bought our first jockstraps and the guy at the store asked, 'Small, medium, or large?' I thought he meant my poor little wee-wee."

"I don't even know what kind to buy."

"Goodyear. It's a name you can trust. And just play it straight. Stay away from the ribbed models and anything in six exciting colors."

"Don't worry."

"Oh, and the novelty items. Tommy Thompson had one in gym the other day and it looked like a souvenir from Sea World."

"They aren't hard to use, are they?"

"Can you put on a sock?"

"Where should we go? I feel like driving into Kansas City, where nobody knows me."

"How about Gent's Pharmacy?"

"Gee, I've known Mr. Gent all my life."

"So what? He's a pro, Walker. He isn't going to call your mom."

Downtown Bradleyville was slowly dying out. The Westgate Mall had taken a lot of business, and if Rachel's father could buy up enough land fast enough, there would be another one to siphon off what was left. Malls like bookends. Stereo malls.

In the Toggery stood the same mannequins that had been there as long as I could remember. At night someone changed their clothes, discreetly drawing a green curtain around them like an aide bathing the elderly. Then they appeared the next day, always dressed, it seemed, in last year's fashions.

At the pharmacy, there was some kid that could have been me ten years ago, reading a comic book featuring

Casper, the Friendly Ghost. There were the same hot-water bottles and enema bags.

"Should we browse," asked Sully, "casually buying a thermos, a chaise lounge, two Ace combs, and oh, yeah, by the way, a dozen rubbers?"

I took a deep breath. "Let's get this over with."

Mr. Gent stood behind the counter like a pastor, both hands balanced on their fingertips. He even remembered my name, and he called Sully *Gerald.*

I asked for twelve of his best prophylactics.

"What?" He actually cupped his ear like an old codger in a bad movie.

"Terrific," I muttered to Sully. "Here we stand in the middle of downtown Bradleyville at four o'clock in the afternoon, shouting about rubbers."

Sully reached for a pad and pencil. "I'll write him a note."

Mr. Gent unfolded the yellow paper and frowned. "What do you boys want these for?"

"For the prevention of disease only, sir," Sully answered.

He snapped open a small bag, the same kind he used to put our penny candy in. Then he turned around, one hand poised like a symphony conductor.

"Don't you want to tell him your brand?"

"I'm not going to smoke them, Gerald."

"We'll have to check these things out. They're probably part of the original shipment from when he opened in 1912."

"Well, let's do it somewhere besides here, okay?"

"Walker, you can't bring them back, you know. They're like swimsuits."

Mr. Gent put the package on the counter and I paid him. "Just a minute," he said, returning my change. Sully and I looked at each other apprehensively. Then he reached into a box with these words on it: *For Good Little Boys and Girls.* A Tootsie Pop for each of us: one lemon, one cherry.

I was flattered when Rachel picked up the phone on the second ring, and even more flattered when she didn't even wait for a hello but asked, "Walker?"

"How did you know?"

"I wanted it to be you. Is everything okay?"

"Sure. My mom still has this cold, but she went to work anyway."

"So, should I come over?"

"I guess I was thinking she might get worse and come home early."

"Doesn't she know we're going to study together?"

"Oh, sure," I lied.

"I'd just leave if she wanted to go to sleep."

I was really getting nervous; the phone was slippery as a trout. Childhood began to look a lot better. I felt like a reluctant immigrant gazing back toward the peaceful countryside of his native land.

"Watch for me, okay? I'm not sure I can find your place in the dark. Blink your porch light."

"Wait, it's —" But she hung up. I went to the window immediately, half expecting to see neighbors lining the streets with cameras and notebooks.

I was sure I should take a shower: if you can't be anything else, be clean, I guess. In the bathroom I looked at myself in the mirror. God, my legs were so white compared to the rest of me. On a pet that would have been considered interesting markings; on a human I wasn't so sure. I was afraid Rachel would take one look at me and just crack up, but short of redwood deck stain, there was nothing I could do.

I stood in the shower and washed everything. I'd seen a movie where people exposed to radioactivity were scrubbed by experts until they almost cried. I made that look like a mother's caress. Then I brushed my teeth six or seven times and stepped back to inspect myself.

It was hot in the bathroom and I was sweating. When I practiced a winning smile, my teeth were pink; I'd brushed too hard and my gums were bleeding. So there I was, multi-colored, dripping wet, and leering like a vampire.

Then I didn't know what to wear. Men in old movies have silk dressing gowns; I had a robe I hadn't worn in years, with Scooby-Doo on the back. I certainly couldn't greet her in a suit; the only one I owned Mom had bought me for my father's funeral. Looking at it hanging there made my chest ache. Maybe I could burst into tears, too. And sweat like a beer stein. And bleed from the gums. I wouldn't need a prophylactic. I *was* birth control. No sensible woman would come within half a mile of me.

I settled for jeans and a T-shirt, and just in time, too. I'd no more than stationed myself at the front window when I saw Rachel's car creeping down the street with only its parking lights on. Every few yards or so she beeped the horn. She couldn't have been more conspicuous if she'd had sirens and a gong.

I turned on the porch light, stood in the open door, and waved. Up the walk she came, carrying an armload of books.

"Hi, sailor," she said.

"Very funny." We linked our arms around one another's waists and kissed, clumsy as second cousins.

I closed the door behind us. "Your house looks bigger," she said.

"My mother's not here. Mothers take up an incredible amount of space."

"Where should I put my books?"

161

"On the bed."

"What bed?"

"Couch. I meant couch."

"You built a fire. It's nice."

All the better to warm you with. I felt like a toothy old wolf.

Rachel settled down to read. Absently she chewed her lower lip as she concentrated; I wanted to chew it, too. Idly she scratched her knee: I wanted to scratch it. Occasionally she glanced at me and smiled as I sat there clutching a magazine like I was in the dentist's office. Finally I couldn't stand it any longer.

"I don't want to study!" I shouted.

"God, Walker." She put her hand to her throat. "You scared me."

"I got you over here on false pretenses."

"I know," she said, smiling.

"I bought prophylactics and everything."

"I bought something, too. Some kind of foam."

"Really?"

"Peggy went with me."

"Sully went with me. Where did you go?"

"The mall. I brought it along, just in case we didn't spend all our time studying."

I moved closer to her. "I had to tell you. I couldn't just start in kissing. It felt too creepy."

162

"I like it this way. It's honest." She took a deep breath. "I'm scared."

"Me too. A little."

"Your mom won't come home, will she?"

"It's a million to one. She's probably onstage right now."

"On what stage?"

"Pardon me?"

"What stage is your mom on right now?"

"Did I say that? I meant on call."

"Like a nurse?"

"More like a bartender on call during that stage of the evening when it's really busy." Lying regularly was certainly making me clever; I would probably grow up and sell used cars.

"I have to use this," she said, opening her purse. I heard the rattle of paper. Then out came something white.

"God, it's huge."

"This is my kitchen timer. We have to wait fifteen minutes." Then she handed me the product.

"Why unicorns?"

"They all had either unicorns on the front or flowers." She stood up and smoothed her skirt demurely. "I guess I'll go to the bathroom. Will you be here?"

"My bedroom's right down the hall."

"Okay. I'll meet you there."

* * *

She appeared in the bedroom door, turned the short fat arrow of the timer to 15, and put it on the dresser.

"Now we have to wait."

"We could rest," I said, making room for her on the bed. I'd turned the sheets back already, partly to hide the Batman spread. Above us hung a P-47 my father had helped me build, and it moved in the sweet evening breeze: rock-a-bye-baby.

"I like your airplane," she said.

"Thank you."

We lay side by side for a while, staring up, arms crossed on our chests like Mr. and Mrs. Dracula.

"Do you want to use what you brought?"

"Isn't the cream enough?"

"I wouldn't want anything to happen. My dad would go crazy."

I'd hidden my purchase deep in my sock drawer. As I searched, the clock ticked relentlessly. I could have been on some sleazy cable game show called "Find the Condom."

"It looks funny," she said when I showed her one. "Like a huge lozenge."

"You have to take the foil off." I showed her.

"And then what?"

I glanced over to see if she was serious. Then I looked at the timer on my dresser. There it stood, next to a picture of me and my folks. I was six and sitting on the traditional pony.

"Would it help to take our clothes off?"

"I think so."

"I don't have very big breasts," she said.

"Neither do I."

"I just mean this is different than the car. This is the real thing. We're going to see each other."

"My stomach is soft," I said.

"Your stomach is nice; I remember."

"I remember your breasts, too."

Rachel calmly started to unbutton her blouse.

"Do you want me to turn my back?" I said.

"Do you want to?"

"God, no."

There was the rustle and whisper of clothes. I couldn't believe it: everything I'd ever dreamed of. A real girl undressing in my bedroom.

"Now you."

"I'm brown on top," I explained, "but my legs are white."

"Like dessert." She held the covers for me and I slipped in beside her.

"They're even smaller," she said, peering down at her chest, "when I'm lying down."

"My stomach is flatter like this. If there was a way to go to high school lying down, I think I'd do it."

She peered over me at the clock. "Just a couple of minutes now. Shouldn't you get ready?"

"Okay," I said reluctantly. But oh, what a sad affair. Above me hung the airplane, below lay Batman, and beyond, the ticking clock as I chased my penis. I thought of Mr. Kramer: had he ever tried to stuff a gander into a stocking?

"Oh, God," I said, falling back in despair. "It's not fair. I've had a million boners I didn't need, and now . . ."

"You're nervous. Peggy said boys get nervous sometimes."

"I don't know what to do," I said helplessly. I even had my forearms crossed across my face like a martyr. Saint Softy, who died for love.

"Let me," she said. "Maybe I know."

"Oh, my God," she said. I smoothed her damp hair. "Oh, my God. It was wonderful. Wasn't it wonderful?"

"Yes."

"You were wonderful."

"No, you were." I tucked the sheet around her so she wouldn't catch cold.

166

"No, no, no. You. I thought I'd died and gone to heaven." She stroked my shoulder. "Are you cold? You're sweating."

"I'm fine. I've never felt better in my life."

"My God." She was just breathless. "No wonder everybody talks about it. It's wonderful. Did you know how wonderful it could be?"

"No," I said, grinning at her.

"The funny thing is that I don't remember very much except that it was wonderful."

"I know. It was pretty mysterious."

"Does it always feel so wonderful?"

"I don't know. It's my second time, too."

"My God, we could do it again, couldn't we?"

I took her hand and showed her. "Yes," I said proudly.

"Wow. I just meant sometime." She glanced down. "Can anybody do that?"

"I don't know," I said happily.

Just then we heard a car turn into the driveway.

"Oh, my God," we said in unison.

Had my mother relapsed? Had she fled the stage, feverishly driving home in her costume? Would she come sneezing and hacking through the front door dressed like some harem pushover, and find us sitting up in bed, barely covered by Robin the Boy Wonder?

Then it was gone; merely somebody turning around. "Maybe we'd better get dressed."

We walked arm in arm to the front door. I was feeling a little sad that she had to go. It'd been great being alone together; now I knew what Tommy Thompson was talking about. Still, I didn't feel like I had scored with Rachel or got her or nailed her or any of the other charming phrases I'd heard Tommy toss around. I just felt close to her. She was — corny as this sounds — dear to me, and I felt privileged to have made love. Jesus, imagine airing those views while the wet towels popped in the locker room. Somebody would take away my Guy badge.

"You wouldn't," Rachel said, leaning on the door, "tell anybody, would you?"

"No, honest."

"Not even Sully?"

Oh. "Not if you don't want me to."

"Did you say you would?"

"Sort of. Not about you, though. Just in general."

"I'm not ashamed or anything," she said quickly.

"No, me neither."

"I just don't want everybody in town to know, everybody including my dad."

I thought about Mom. I wondered if the condom I

had thrown in the toilet had gone down, or if it was still floating there like some weird sea creature.

Rachel put her arms around me and hugged. Hard.

"Peggy really likes Sully," she said. "But she's afraid that he doesn't want to be with her because of the way she's been."

"Well, Sully's afraid that she'll laugh at him because he's never done it."

"How many people in the world," she said reflectively, "are doing it right now, do you think?"

"Everywhere in the world? It must be millions."

Her eyes widened. "Millions. Wow. And if most of them smoke afterward, no wonder there's smog." She opened the door and peeked out. "I guess I'll just march right down the walk like nothing happened."

"You look pretty happy."

"Maybe your neighbors will think I finally finished my term paper."

"They're probably asleep."

"Are you going to tell your mom I was here studying?"

I shook my head.

"Me neither. Dad thinks I'm at the library. God, if every kid who said he was going to the library actually went, they'd have to send out for more books." She kissed me lightly, took two steps, then turned. The porch light made her hair glow. "I'm glad you were the one."

"I'm glad you were, too."

Sully and I were standing by my locker. Taped inside the door was a picture of a bright green John Deere tractor he'd cut out of some feed and grain catalog as a joke. Past him I could see other doors, and inside them long photos of girls with impossibly big breasts, their eyes half-closed in routine pinup ecstasy.

"Should I have told her about Mom right then?" I asked. "I mean, did I miss the opportunity of a lifetime?"

He stroked his chin like a thoughtful actor in a mystery.

"My dad says everybody lies sometimes. Even animals. Possums lie; they aren't dead. Blowfish lie; they aren't that big and tough."

"Pretty fast crowd I'm in — possums and blowfish."

"Dad says you can't tell the truth all the time, anyway. You have to wait or you'll just confuse people or hurt their feelings."

"Okay, but what happens when Mr. Gardner wants us all to come to Thanksgiving dinner, and there Mom sits in her G-string with her snake?"

He took a step back. "She's got a snake?"

I waved that away. "I don't know."

"What would she want a snake for?"

"Forget it, okay? It was a bad example."

"Look, your mom's been cool so far. Why would she blow the whistle now, all of a sudden?"

I raised my palms helplessly. "It's not really about her. It's about me. I really just want to tell Rachel, but there never seems to be a good time."

"Forget about it. Maybe it's like my dad says about diseases. Left alone, ninety percent of them just go away."

"And the other ten?"

He shrugged. "I guess you die."

chapter **4**

OF course, no one died. In fact, going with Rachel just got sweeter and deeper and richer. A week or so later, I was out at the Land Time Forgot (or, to be completely fair, the Land Dad Forgot). There wasn't that much to do, really; everything was coming up on its own, but I liked being there by myself. I had a hoe and a big old heavy rake with dragon's teeth for tines, and I strolled up and down the rows like the shoppers who would eventually take over. Except that I was on the lookout for bindweed, mallow, and fescue.

I could still lose myself out there, even without the noise the tractor. It was a little like going diving —

something Dad and I had done when we all went to Florida — being alone in all that deep silence. Occasionally as I worked, a mermaid would float by (that would be Rachel) or a shark (my physics final) or something like my mom (pretty but baffling). Mostly, though, it was just me moving slowly, happy by myself, hacking at the scrappy weeds, getting sunburned: the Farmer in the Mall.

Then, when I looked up, there were my friends in Sully's mom's convertible. They all waved; Rachel stood on the seat and shouted my name. Sully held up a picnic basket. I could see Peggy grin, both arms in the air like a lottery winner.

I pulled on a shirt as Rachel kissed me lightly. I probably had less of a stomach than before, and it was even more tanned — not so much like Moby-Dick's nose — but I still felt better covering it up.

"What's the occasion?" I asked, looking at the food.

Rachel shrugged. "I ran into Peggy at the mall, she called Sully, and presto."

Sully looked around. "It's great out here. I'm so sick of studying." He began to box, throwing little pitty-pat combinations first at nobody, then at me. "Maybe I could become Gerald the Fighting Psychiatrist. A sign on my couch would read GET WELL OR ELSE." Then he hit me hard enough to sting and took off running.

We raced to the nearest fencerow, then turned,

panting. Looking back, I watched Rachel and Peggy hold the checkered cloth taut, raise it till it filled with the warm spring air, then kneel and cover the soft earth at the edge of the field. Rachel opened a basket, and Peggy held out her hands for the napkins and for plates so shiny they reflected the sun.

"They're really women, aren't they, Sully?"

"Are you kidding? One of them's wearing raccoon makeup and a man's sport coat made into a skirt; the other one looks like she just stepped out of *Seventeen.*"

"I know, but they still seem more grown-up than I feel."

"Girls have always seemed about three years ahead of me for as long as I can remember. And speaking of being a kid, I guess I'm not one anymore."

"You're kidding."

"Couple of nights ago. But don't let on. Peggy asked me not to tell."

"Rachel too." We were shaking hands and grinning like we'd just closed some stupendous deal.

"I was so scared," he said. "And it wasn't anything like those X-rated movies we saw in Love's Park where the guy is always leering and sweating. First of all, it just kind of happened all on its own."

"God, I know that one."

"You too?"

"The first time, yeah."

"The first time? Are you still doing it?"

"Not right now. I'm talking to you; this is *social* inter-course, remember."

Sully laughed a little nervously, then got quiet again. I knew he had more on his mind.

"I really like Peggy," he said intently. "She's so . . ." He squinted and looked west, as if the word were written on the horizon. "Kind," he said finally. "She's really got a good heart. I mean, sure it comes naturally and all that, but I was still really clumsy and she made me feel like a goddamned king."

We were leaning on a rail fence, a real one. I don't think Lincoln had split the logs or anything, but somebody a long time ago had worked hard on them. I moved my arm so our elbows touched and Sully grinned up at me.

"What's it like the second time?"

"Different. Better in a way, naturally. We've got all this birth control stuff, so —"

"What do you guys use?"

"Everything. What about you?"

He shrugged. "I guess I thought that Peggy was on the pill."

"Probably."

"Still, I'd better check. My dad says sperm are really tricky devils."

I shook my head. "All that crap you hear about in health ed. about the awesome responsibility that goes along with sex turns out to be true."

"I used to think that if I was a surgeon instead of a shrink, I'd give anybody an abortion anytime she wanted one. Now I'm not so sure. I mean, is that any way to make a living?"

"How about plastic surgery."

"Isn't that a lie? You're not young; you just look young."

I waved my hand at him, palm flat. "Plastic surgery is okay. It's in the Bible, in the Lost Cosmetic Scrolls. 'Thou shalt lift thy jowls if thou wantest to and thy behind also may be hoisted, sometimes in lean years, sometimes in fat.'"

He laughed at my nonsense, then turned around, resting his elbows on the rough wood like some guy at a bar.

"Look at them," he said. "God, they're our girl-friends. I never had a girlfriend before."

"They're waving to us," I said. "Let's go eat."

"Do you guys do it a lot?"

"Sure," I said. "I eat lunch every day."

Full of tuna salad and Ruffles, the heavenly taste of choco-late cake still in my mouth, Rachel's hand on mine, the sun pouring down on everything, me feeling happy and safe and content: we lay down — moving some things aside, putting others away — with all our heads together and our feet pointing off in the four directions of the compass.

"I don't know," said Peggy, talking so slow and thick it was like she was half asleep or hypnotized, "maybe Walker's right, you guys."

"Walker's always right," said Rachel, just as slowly.

"What am I right about this time?" I asked, imagining that instead of tumbling out all edges and points, the nouns and verbs floated up slowly into the gorgeous blue sky, followed by the articles and prepositions just tagging along.

"This place," Peggy said. "It's fabulous out here. I'd kind of hate to see it swallowed up by Toys R Us and the Hair Affair."

"You guys should see a great mall," Rachel said dreamily.

"You wouldn't miss this place?" Sully asked, trying to balance a Ruffle on his nose.

Rachel took a long, luxurious breath and let it out. "Don't get me wrong. Part of me doesn't want to see this disappear, either. I just mean it'd be nice for you guys to see a great mall, that's all." She reached for a carrot stick, then held it between her index and middle fingers. "It's too bad you can't smoke vegetables," she mused.

"Where is this great mall?" I murmured. "We'll go." I

turned my face toward Rachel's, nuzzling into her dark hair until I could feel her skin. She smelled, of all things, like papaya.

"Manoa Marketplace," she said. "But that's in Hawaii."

"Aloha," said Sully. "Which means hello, goodbye, and charge it."

"The Houston Galleria, Faneuil Hall, Ghirardelli Square," Rachel recited. She had her hands folded primly on her tummy and she looked like a little girl who had fainted during a recitation but bravely continued.

"Can we drive to any of those? I have to be home for dinner."

"The Emerald City's not bad."

"Said Dorothy to her new friends."

"Where's that?"

"It's in Love's Park, about an hour from here."

"Then we should go," Peggy said languidly.

"We should," Sully added. He was smoking a carrot stick, elaborately tapping the make-believe ashes in my face. "These aren't bad," he mused, "but they're not a man's smoke. 'I'd walk a kilometer for a carrot' doesn't cut it."

"I need a kiss," said Rachel. "Just a tiny one."

"Kiss Rachel," I said to Sully. "You're closer."

"No, no, no." She shook her head lazily. "Sully has vegetable breath. It would be like kissing a relish tray. You kiss me."

"I smell like cake."

"Good."

"I could go to a mall," Peggy said. "I need some shoes." Her sentence floated skyward, lazy as incense.

"They only sell red shoes in the Emerald City Mall."

"When should we go?"

"Saturday?"

"Are we serious about this?"

All our heads nodded simultaneously.

"You know," said Peggy, "this is like a movie."

"Four Kids Lying on the Ground. I saw it."

"No, a really old movie where the camera is like on the ceiling and you look down on these girls and they're all doing the same synchronized movements?"

"Busby Berkeley," said Sully.

"Yes. Let's do it. Everybody hold hands and put your arms back and your legs apart and we'll make a star."

We followed Peggy's directions, goofing around and laughing. I don't know if we looked like a star. What I do know is that when Peggy wanted us to make a snowflake she had us all lift one leg and point our toes, and her skirt and Rachel's slid down. All of a sudden there were their long legs and I got this really embarrassing erection and probably destroyed the pattern completely. I mean, whoever heard of a snowflake with a boner?

Luckily Sully got tired of it or embarrassed or maybe he had a little problem of his own; anyway, he started to tickle Peggy and she rolled into him, pinning his arms to his side.

Just then Mr. Kramer's car turned off the main road and rattled our way. We watched without saying anything as he cruised right up next to us. We all waved, brushed off our clothes, and stood up.

When Mr. Kramer got out, he touched the brim of his hat, called Rachel ma'am, and asked me how I'd been. I said all right.

"Well, I just came by to see how things looked. I'm on my way over to take some things to my oldest boy. Keepsakes," he said softly, "and things like that."

Rachel glanced at the car. "Can I see?" she asked. "Would you mind? I like old things."

"Help yourself."

As she leaned into the little gray Chevy, he and I walked toward the field where the very first oats had taken hold but not prospered. They weren't even green like the others, but yellow like a porch light.

"I talked to your mother," he said, looking straight ahead like a sea captain. "Did she tell you?"

"Not really. She's got this weird schedule and we don't always see each other."

"What it comes down to, I guess, is Rachel's daddy got a little high and mighty with her."

"With Mom? About what?"

"This here." He pointed. "Gardner's under the gun a little, the way I hear it. Now the city council's dragging their heels on all the zoning he needs, not just this piece here. I think if he could get one of us to do something definite, he hopes the rest would just line up."

"Are you going to sell?"

"Don't know. Funny thing is, we could almost have our cake and eat it. If we sold tomorrow, we'd see this fall and another spring before the machines moved in. Hell, we could lease your place and that section of mine for grazing and turn a nice profit."

"Enough to pay for college?"

"Enough to get you in the front door."

"Do you trust him?" I glanced toward Rachel, who was absorbed in a large cardboard box.

"Far enough to take his money. Mostly I feel sorry for him. Used to be men come to town before the circus. They'd put up posters and sell tickets and then be gone before the elephants ever set foot on Main Street. Always wondered if they ever saw the show." He shook his head. "Hell of a way to live."

Rachel walked over to us holding a long album with a thick imitation-leather cover.

"Are these you when you were young?" she asked.

Mr. Kramer turned the long, dark pages, soft as a spaniel's ears. Four tiny chevrons held each picture in place, and the first few were all of women standing beside huge automobiles — Hudsons, a Nash Ambassador, Packards. There was always a mountain in the background or the first fifteen feet of a famous tree.

"Now," said Mr. Kramer, pointing to a big horse, "that's Prince and that there's Speedy Boy." His fingers moved lightly in all directions, like he was winning at checkers. "This is old Dutch and over here is Pal, Waymond's little dog, and that heifer with the blaze face is June. Mattie cried when the truck came, but she brought near forty dollars a hundred, and we almost had to have the money."

There was a baby picture of Wilson, their oldest, seated by a chicken bigger than he was; one of a startled Pal next to Waymond fixed up to look like a cat, with whiskers radiating like spokes from his mouth, a union suit dyed black, and a long piece of rope for a tail; and finally a color photo of someone standing solemnly beside his first rifle.

Then there were large photographs of country

schools with names like Denton and Grass Valley; comic postcards that all featured outhouses and dazed, bosomy Ozark gals in tattered shorts; and family reunion pictures — Mr. Kramer pointed and named everyone.

"Iris just wasted away and that's a fact; Edith had the dropsy, Hilda and Evelyn both took to drink, and Lula lives in Washington, D.C., with a black man; Eda just dropped dead one day opening a can of Maxwell House coffee; Loy there went to Vietnam and when he came back, he just wasn't right, though he's awful good with his hands and he can fix anything."

"You've lived here a long time, haven't you?" Rachel asked quietly.

"All my life."

"God, that sounds great: I've stayed in a lot of big cities, but this is the first place I've ever really lived."

Later on, Sully and Peggy followed Mr. Kramer out toward the main road. He drove like a lot of old guys, leaning right up against the wheel, using both hands like he was steering a four-master. Behind him Sully lounged in the big convertible, Peggy's head on his shoulder, his arm around her, steering with one finger.

I helped Rachel fold up the plaid blanket, and without saying anything, we headed for the oak like we'd done a dozen times before, always carefully picking our way among the tender shoots.

"What'll your dad do if all the people he needs to sell don't sell and if all the places he needs rezoned don't get rezoned?"

"He'll build something else," she said. "He's tried to get the Garden of Gardner up before, you know."

"What does he build instead?"

"It depends on the financing. Pretty much whatever he can. Dad's realistic. If he can't get what he wants, he takes what he can get and moves on."

He sounded like Attila the Hun, but I didn't say that.

"I thought you weren't going to move anymore."

Rachel leaned to smooth the blanket she'd laid out.

"He moves on in his mind. He's not a kid, in other words. He doesn't pout. If people say, 'We don't want your Garden,' he says, 'Okay, what do you want?'"

I sat down beside her, then got right back up again and took off my shirt. I have to admit I was getting vain about my suntan, and I was a lot less shy about my stomach. Okay, it wasn't a plane of rippling flesh, but it wasn't like I couldn't see the ground.

"I like you with your shirt off," Rachel said.

"I like you with your shirt off, too."

"Want me to?" she said impishly.

"Right here?"

She nodded, grinning. "Should I?"

"Rachel, I'm sixteen. I'm at my sexual peak. If I don't say yes now, I have to go to a monastery."

She undid one button, then pulled the blouse over her head. "Hi, motorists," she said, waving to the distant highway. "Hi, Reverend Falwell; hi, Father Murphy." Then she turned her back to me. "Help me with this, okay?"

I had a little attack of performance anxiety, but I took a deep breath and started in. Rachel squirmed a little.

"Does this have a combination or something?"

"I'll do it."

I sat down with a thump. "God, Sully and I saw these movies once and every guy in them could take a girl's bra off with one hand."

"I saw one of those. We sneaked into this sleazo theater in Miami. All the girls had these enormous breasts." She stared down at herself. "Do boys really like humongous ones?"

"I don't know. Everybody's worried about something. Guys are worried about having a little wiener."

"I know. Tommy Thompson's is supposed to be little."

I sat up. "No kidding! God, wait till I tell Sully. That's the best news I've heard in a long time."

"Well, I like my breasts," she said, "just the way they are." She stroked one tenderly, like it was a puppy. Then frowned. "Look, a pimple."

I leaned toward the tiny spot.

"Don't," she said. "It's icky."

I shook my head.

"Are you sure?" she asked.

"Yes." I could feel the warmth of her perfect flesh, then one hand on the back of my head as she pulled me to her.

The funny thing is that we didn't make love, not that day, anyway. And that was the answer to Sully's question, Do you guys do it a lot? I mean, the answer is yes and no. Sometimes it was just as nice to only touch each other and kiss. That's what we did that afternoon, getting lully and woozy with those long, oasis-type kisses, then just drifting off to sleep.

"God," Rachel said, sitting up, "I drooled."

I untangled myself. It sounds romantic to sleep in one another's arms, but not when something goes numb. Like my right hand. I shook it violently as she dressed. Her bra wouldn't go on right and something of my own was tangled, too. With my live hand I reached into my jeans.

"Walker, what's it like to have a penis?"

"It's handy. This way I don't look different in gym class."

"I've always wondered. I think I secretly want one."

"Christmas is a long way off. Are you hinting for your birthday?"

"It must be so weird to have this thing hanging off you."

"I feel that way about your breasts. I always thought that if I had a pair I'd always be touching them."

"Do you touch your thing much?"

"Just to go to the bathroom and at night when I put a sock on it."

"You're kidding. A sock?" She looked like I'd just told her that I breathed through my feet.

"So it won't catch cold when I'm asleep. When it catches cold it sneezes, and if I'm in class and my pants jump I get embarrassed."

Rachel began to beat on me with both fists, but lightly.

"I like you so much, Walker," she said, getting serious all of a sudden. "I told Peggy I did, and she said to tell you."

"Thanks, Peggy."

"She's funny, isn't she?"

"How do you mean?" I stooped to help Rachel with our things.

"She has this terrible reputation but she's really nice."

"Maybe a lot of that is just talk."

She shook her head. "Nope. Peggy told me. I just used to think that somebody who got around like that would have to be a prostitute or a stripper or something. Now I know better."

"Strippers aren't the same as prostitutes," I said supercasually.

"I guess not. Anyway, Peggy's nice, and I'm glad we're friends."

Rachel was tucked in under my right arm. I could feel her as we walked together. Her hair tickled a little under my chin and I could still hear her saying that she liked me so much.

What would happen if I told her I knew a stripper? Really knew one. Would she get cold immediately just like the freeze that supposedly finished off the dinosaurs? Would she slip out from under my arm for good? Would the terrific kissing stop?

"Are you okay?" she asked softly. "What are you thinking about?"

"I've got a little chill, I guess. Maybe I'm catching cold."

I stayed home from school for a day, sneezed, slept, and looked out the window. It had begun to rain, so light sometimes it seemed to barely flicker, so heavy at others that I wondered if the oats could stand up under it.

Rachel got assignments from my teachers and phoned them in, while Sully gave me the standard lecture on psychosomatic illness: I wasn't really ill, he said, just guilty and scared. So I blew my nose into the phone.

Mom was really nice, moving the TV in from the living room, bringing me hot tomato soup, and regularly putting her cool hand on my forehead.

"I'm going to bring a friend of mine home from work tonight," she said, sitting down on the edge of the bed. "You can come out and say hi if you're up to it, but you don't have to, okay?"

I nodded as slightly as possible, like the Godfather, but it was supposed to mean tons.

"He's a nice guy. I think you'll like him."

"Is he married?"

"Divorced."

"Are you going to marry him?"

"I don't know."

"Has he got a name?"

"Rocco. But I call him Rocks."

"You're kidding." I almost spilled my soup.

"Yes, I'm kidding. His name is Porter."

"That's handy. He can carry your bags when you run away together."

"Does anybody tell you how good you look lately? Does Rachel tell you?"

"I lost a little weight while I was working with Mr. Kramer."

And then she did a funny thing. She picked my hand up off of Batman's cape and kissed it. It was very gallant.

"I like you, too," I said, swallowing hard. "And it's okay to bring your boyfriends home. Better here than out necking where the cops will pick you up and I'll have to drive down to the station and bail you out of jail."

She smiled again, lighting up the gloom. "We'll be back around ten-thirty. Will you be okay? There's about a thousand gallons of soup on the stove." She got to her feet, then turned and looked critically at me. "We've got to get you a new bedspread. Something a little more grown-up."

On Saturday, Sully picked me up for our field trip to the Emerald City Mall. As we drove toward Peggy's, I assured him that I was hale and hearty, and I told him about my mom's date.

"So did you meet him?"

"I staggered out in my pajamas. He was just this guy. I thought he'd have two or three gold chains and cufflinks as big as hubcaps, but he was wearing this kind of geeky sport shirt and he was going bald."

"So what did they do?"

"I didn't hang around very long, but I think they just drank some wine and talked. I could hear my mom giggling."

"That's all?"

"They never left the living room and she walked him to the door about midnight. I heard her lock up and go to bed."

"Things are really working out well, aren't they? I mean with you and your mom and you and Rachel. . . ."

"And you and Peggy."

"Yeah," he said, grinning. "God, I'm happy, Walker. I'm really happy."

"Me too. I'd be a little happier if I could come clean with Rachel, though. About my mom."

"Give yourself some time. She's probably got some secrets too, you know?"

"I think about telling her all the time, but . . . Look, if I told her this morning, what could happen? I'd just screw up the whole day for everybody, right?"

"That's a strong possibility."

"See? If we're getting along great, I don't want to ruin it. If we're not getting along so hot, I don't want to make things worse."

He pulled up in front of Peggy's duplex and turned off the engine. "Look, there'll be a good time. I know it."

"When, I wonder."

"That," he said, climbing out, "I don't know."

The trip into the city was really nice. Rachel looked just great. She'd had Peggy put streaks in her hair and sweep it back, so she looked very speedy.

Sully had the top of his mom's convertible down, and the sun was out. When we passed the oats, they were tall enough to wave in the breeze, and Rachel said hello and waved back.

There was one sticky minute when we got into the suburb of Love's Park: a giant billboard advertised Ye Olde Burlesque.

"You know," said Peggy, "that's supposed to be a pretty good show. Pretty funny and kind of family-oriented and . . ."

Rachel, who was looking the other way, just smiled politely.

"Thanks," I mouthed to Peggy, who smiled and shrugged.

We walked — four abreast, arms linked just like in the movie — into the Emerald City, following, of course, a winding road that started with a single yellow brick in the parking lot and grew until we reached the towering entrance.

"Tell me the truth," said Rachel. "Don't you think it's kind of exciting?"

She drew us all to one side, away from the cataract of shoppers, away from the Munchkins clapping their gloved hands and pointing little kids toward the Tin Man and beyond him the Cowardly Lion and finally the Scarecrow, each one drawing the families deeper and deeper into the mall.

"Just listen for a minute," Rachel advised. Grinning at each other, we cocked our heads. Sure enough: there was the surfy hiss of money changing hands, an occasional yelp or muffled name, and — my God — the footsteps. I remembered how my dad had told me that in the army soldiers broke ranks to cross a bridge because all that left-right-left stuff could shake it to pieces. I imagined I could feel the mall tremble and thought I could see the imperceptible shudder of the fixtures.

Rachel led us into the flux. "No cars," she said, pointing like a tour guide, "no trams, nothing bigger or stronger than a person."

"So people feel safe?" asked Sully.

"Right."

"Safe enough to buy," I added sardonically.

"God, I already want something," Peggy exclaimed.

"What?"

"Anything, everything. I don't care."

We strolled down a mild incline.

"What's way down at the end?" I asked. "Oz's castle?"

Rachel thought for a second. "Neiman Marcus, I think." And when I laughed, she did, too.

We passed Interior Systems, B. Dalton, Chrome Concepts, On Stage, Digital Den, and Noah's Ark Pet Center.

"Some mall somewhere," explained Rachel, "has a House of Nose Jobs."

"Does their ad say, 'Come in and pick your nose'?" asked Sully.

We took a break in the central court, sitting beside a Munchkin holding his costumed stomach. Three stories up, a huge dome let in the light. Rachel checked her copy of the *Emerald News,* a one-page newspaper thrust into every hand by a fairly surly dwarf.

"It's almost time," she said.

"For what?"

"Watch," and she rolled her eyes skyward.

Just then the Muzak was interrupted by recorded trumpets. The fanfare was elaborate, and I looked around for Dorothy and Toto.

Instead, high above us, the dome cracked and rolled slowly back. There were the frothy mares' tails and the endless blue.

"Ladies and gentlemen," intoned Sully, "Emerald City Mall proudly presents the weather."

For a moment the whole place was nearly silent. Thousands of shoppers paused and tilted their heads back like they all needed eyedrops. Then someone moved, a child cried, the Muzak came on with a groan, and the moment was over.

"Do you guys want to shop?" asked Peggy, looking feverish.

Sully and I looked at each other and shook our heads.

"You should shop, Walker. Whose pants are you wearing?"

I looked down, too, half embarrassed. "Either my clothes are growing or I'm shrinking."

Peggy took Rachel's hand. "We'll do it for you. We'll scope out the best stores. Give us half an hour. Meet us by the Wicked Witch of the West." Then they were gone.

On our own, Sully and I stepped into the human stream and let it carry us along. We swept past Slack Shack, Cinema VI, Foot Locker, Lady Foot Locker, and Harrison's Hats.

"I can't help it," Sully said. "I want something."

"God, me too. It's probably against the law to be empty-handed in here."

"How about this?" He pointed to a pink neon sign, and like weary salmon we slipped into the quiet pool of A Luv Pub.

"Gentlemen," said a tall brunette in a camouflage-patterned jumpsuit trimmed in rhinestones. She looked like she was ready to parachute into Beverly Hills.

"We just came in," I said, "to get out of the rain." But I didn't get a glimmer out of her.

"Let me know if I may be of any help." She played that little tune like a doorbell.

"Imagine coming home to her," I said.

"Imagine coming home to that." Sully pointed to a mannequin in long stockings with garters and some kind of weird panties.

"Are those torn," he asked, "or do they come that way?"

"They sure look drafty."

On the wall hung long negligees, goofy little bras that looked like architecture projects in minimum lift, and every conceivable combination of strap and truss, all done in lace and leather. They looked frilly but uncomfortable.

"Oh, God," I said, gaping at set after set of tassels attached to tiny cones.

"At last, something wholesome. Little party hats."

"Do you think my mom has to wear these?"

"Beats me. How do you keep them on, anyway? Bondex?"

Just then, a tired-looking blonde with shopping bags from Nordstrom's led a clerk to the spangly wall, pointed to a pair of golden tassels, examined them critically, then opted for pink.

"She can't be a stripper, too, can she?"

"Even if she is, they can't all be." Sully pointed to the lines at both registers. Most of the women were around my mom's age. Had they really come to the mall to buy a hat, a blender, an oven mitt, and a G-string?

"Would you want Peggy to wear any of this stuff?"

"I don't think so. Would you?"

"Do you think Rachel would want to?"

"Beats me. Maybe you have to be old to get into this stuff."

Luv's commando ambushed us as we left. "Gentlemen," she said, "perhaps next time."

"Roll when you hit the ground," I advised her.

Blank. No response.

Sully pulled me out the door. "Let's go meet the girls."

* * *

They were waiting right under the towering witch, and when Rachel spotted us, she handed her package to Peggy and ran to meet me.

Man, that really got me. I'd never had a girl do that before, throw herself into my arms, I mean, much less in front of a thousand strangers. Nobody seemed to give it a second thought, except maybe a nice smile here and there. Maybe Rachel was right about malls. Maybe they were magical worlds apart.

"It's not so bad, is it?" she asked, just like she could read my mind.

"It's great," I said, holding her tighter.

"I meant the mall," she said, grinning.

"I meant the mall."

Peggy and Sully cruised up beside us. "There's a free show," she said. "Down there at the end of Munchkin Land." She looked at us, question marks in both eyes. "With a stage and everything."

"Why not?"

We slipped into one of the front rows and watched the other shoppers settle, some — like the birds out at my place — circling warily, some swooping right down to squabble over a choice spot.

It really was like downtown used to be, at least in a way. There were lots of old people — some the condo type with white shoes and matching belts, but others like Mr. Kramer, in clean overalls and blue Big Boy work shirts with the top button fastened, sitting patiently holding a straw hat or a cane or their wife's mammoth black purse. On the edge of the crowd stood the mothers with their strollers, moving them back and forth, back and forth, like vacuum cleaners.

Beside me sat a banker type, reeking of English Leather; beside him a woman who kept tugging at her tiny skirt like it had a mind of its own; then a kid with three earrings, Security in his yellow blazer, motor-cyclist, pimply genius, Vietnam vet, lady with a bagel. Just like downtown used to be.

Finally a girl in high heels and a miniature bunny suit featuring a huge cotton puff on her behind tottered out with a placard and balanced it on the easel at the edge of the stage:

MISS MAUREEN'S SCHOOL
OF THE DANCE
TAP, TOE, & JAZZ

Miss Maureen herself — packed into a spandex suit and grinning with only one side of her mouth, like she'd just come from the dentist — introduced the ballet portion.

Nobody could stay on her toes for very long, though, and as they slammed down on their heels, then heaved themselves up again, it looked like a dance celebrating combustion.

Ten kids tapped to "Sunny Side of the Street," and

jazz dancing turned out to be preteens with yards of chiffon tearing around the stage until they all got low-grade fevers and began to bawl.

Still, flashbulbs went off constantly and we clapped along with everybody else, just like the show was going on in the big scalloped bandshell in Bradleyville's park instead of indoors somewhere in a manmade Oz.

Rachel and I held hands most of the time and patiently listened to a singer — a pious girl who sang "My Way" the same way everybody else sings "My Way"— and then a rock band called Cryin' Bob and the Furniture.

"Let's go," said Sully, holding his ears.

"One more," Peggy pleaded. "Please?"

The next act was a magician modestly called Jack the Great. He pulled flowers out of his cape lining, turned ropes into ribbons, and produced a dazed-looking pigeon from a hat. Then he asked for a volunteer from the audience.

"C'mon, folks," he chided.

"You do it, Walker," Peggy said.

"Forget it."

"Here's one!" she shouted.

"Big hand, folks," said Jack, pointing at me.

Rachel urged me. "It'll be fun."

"For who?"

200

Jack held out his hand. Everyone who didn't have to go up there was staring at me like I was a real spoilsport. I climbed the makeshift stairs.

"What's your name?" boomed Jack.

I told him.

"Speak up, Walter. Now, have you ever been a magician's assistant before?"

"No, but I'm not Walter."

"You just said you were."

"*You* just said I was."

Jack looked at the audience. "Is this credibility, folks, or what? Not only does he not know me, he doesn't even know himself."

I started to protest, but Jack was wound up. "Now, Walter, I'd like to talk to you a long time and get to know your hopes and dreams, not to mention your real name, but I've got a show to do here so I'll need your belt."

I looked down. "My belt?"

Jack looked around. "Is there an echo in here? Yes, your belt."

"What about my pants?"

"Please, this is a family show."

"They're a little loose; I lost some weight."

"Just hand over the belt, okay, and while I prepare to dazzle everyone, you can tell us your diet secrets."

I shrugged and took it off. When my pants actually

201

slipped a little, I grabbed for them and the audience laughed.

I looked across the footlights, embarrassed. But everybody was smiling up at me and applauding. They seemed nice, not mean, and I kind of liked it up there. Was this, I wondered, how my mom felt six nights a week?

Jack wrapped my belt around both wrists, then whipped out a pair of handcuffs.

"Tell us," he said as he trussed me up, "how you lost weight. There's a lot of dieters out there, I'll bet."

"Well." I leaned into the mike, but it squealed and I jumped back. "I, uh, started this job and it was kind of hard, so that was part of it. Then I met this really nice girl and I guess I thought she'd like me better if I wasn't fat."

Everything stopped, even Jack. Really embarrassed, I shuffled back a step or two. Then there was this incredible applause. Everybody was clapping and smiling.

"Is she here?" shouted Jack. "Is your girlfriend here? Take a bow, little lady. Stand up."

Now it was Rachel's turn to be shy, but I grinned and motioned with my cuffed hands, and, beaming, she stood, turned around, and waved. Then she smiled at me even though I was holding up my pants with both hands.

chapter 5

"Did I take too long?" asked Sully, sliding in behind the wheel.

"Let's put it this way: you were parked here so long they gave your car a ZIP code."

"You didn't exactly run up to the door with Rachel, then run right back, either."

"I know. It was too nice up there."

"She really loves you, pardner."

"Really?"

"Are you kidding? After that thing in the mall, she didn't take her eyes off you for a minute. I thought she was going to go in the dressing room with you when you were buying those new cords."

"She really was nice today."

"During dinner, during everything. In the movies I looked over and she was still looking at you."

"I wanted to tell her I loved her."

"Why didn't you?"

"Scared, I guess. I never told anybody before."

"Not Debbie?"

I shook my head. "I think Rachel almost told me, too." I glanced over at him. "What do you say to Peggy?"

He looked down at the steering wheel. "We don't talk about that stuff much."

"Well, if Rachel does love me, you know why, don't you?"

"Sure, you're a nice guy."

"No, I mean exactly why. It's because I told the truth."

"About what?"

"About her. When I was up on that stage with Jack the Great and I said how I lost weight."

"She loved that, man."

"It just popped out. And it's the truth. She's why I don't eat like I used to. It hasn't got squat to do with being a field hand."

"Well, it sure did the trick."

I turned in my seat. "Let's go see my mom."

He looked baffled. "I know it's silly to want connections between sentences, but humor me."

"I want to tell Rachel the truth about my mom, too. So I want to go see the place where she works; I want to see her act; I want to see everything and then tell Rachel."

"Are you sure about this?"

"No," I said, and we both laughed. "But let's do it anyway."

He narrowed his eyes. "You could be right. The timing couldn't be better. She's nuts about you."

"Let's go before I lose my nerve."

"Okay, but you need a drink."

"Why?"

"Because John Wayne always had one."

"Before he saw his mother onstage?"

"Before he rode into town to get his cattle back. He had a double whiskey."

"Where are we going to get a double whiskey?"

"Doesn't your mom have some liquor?"

"Just wine."

He frowned. "It'll have to do."

"I thought your mom got home at ten-thirty," Sully said when I climbed back into the car.

"Not this week. She traded with somebody whose father was sick." I handed him a glass.

"Not for me. I'm going to drive; you're going to drink. I don't want to end up with our yearbook pictures on some Teen Alcohol poster. And anyway, don't use a glass. Drink out of the bottle."

I poured some, sloshed it around, and sniffed it like I'd seen my parents do. "But this is how it's done."

"Not when you're pumping up your courage." He nudged the bottom of the bottle.

I took a swallow and grimaced. "An awful little vintage," I said, "with a runny nose and a history of petty crime. Yuck."

Sully was a good driver, and he liked to go fast. Just that afternoon the trip had taken over an hour. That night it took thirty-four minutes.

Once, on the way, he reached over with his free hand and massaged my neck like a trainer loosening up his fighter. Another time he punched me encouragingly.

I wanted to tell him how much I liked it that he was able to do that, how much it helped, and how much I liked him; but I couldn't. Even though that was the truth, too.

When we pulled into the parking lot, I sat up and looked around.

"Not exactly scores of eager valets rushing to serve us," Sully observed.

The place was a dump, a big, seedy roadhouse out in the middle of nowhere. An enormous neon woman towered over it. Every few seconds her neon gown disappeared and there were her neon breasts, capped tastefully with red bulbs that blinked furiously.

"Oh, my God."

We made our way among the cars parked at weird angles, one with the front doors standing open. Was everyone in such a hurry to see my mother that they couldn't park in rows?

"I'm pretty high," I said, bouncing off a fender.

"Good, I've got a hunch you'll need every drop."

We could hear the music, all drums and saxophones.

"Watch your step," Sully cautioned me.

I inched around a piece of plywood thrown across a miniature bog. Lying on it were one high-heeled shoe, half a banana, an empty oil can, and a wrinkled condom.

"I think I saw that in the Museum of Modern Art last year," Sully said. "It was called *The Meaning of Life.*"

"I can't go through with this," I said. "I think I'm having a heart attack."

"Anxiety. I'll get you a paper bag from the waitress and you can breathe into it."

"I can hear it now. 'I'll have a double boilermaker zombie and a lunch bag for my friend.'"

We were almost to the open door when it burst open and out came these extras from *Night of the Slime People*, big hairy guys whose hands hung down past their knees.

They eyed us suspiciously. Sully and I moved closer together, like children in a dark wood. I was more afraid of getting chewed up than beaten up.

Then one gargoyle jerked his thumb toward the door.

"Great," he said in a kind of half yawn, half moo.

"Probably the entertainment editor from the *Times*," said Sully, ushering me inside.

A bored blonde sitting behind a makeshift counter took one look at us.

"ID?"

"Of course," Sully said, whipping out his wallet.

She looked at it, looked at him. She held it at arm's length, then up close like a jeweler. She even took the gum out of her mouth in order to concentrate.

"This isn't the real you," she said.

"Still, it's an interesting question. What is the self, anyway? Or, as you put it so well, 'the real you'? Is it the polite face we all don in the morning, or is there a deeper . . ."

I let Sully yammer while I looked for my mom, steadying myself on the doorjamb.

There was so much smoke it was hard to see, but the woman onstage was no relative of mine. I could hear her shriek even above the kind of drumming that would have sent Tarzan diving under the bed. As I watched, she tore off a hairy bra like it had bit her, raced furiously around the stage, then began to climb the grimy curtain.

How would I tell Rachel about this?

"Fellas, what can I do for you?"

Apparently the hostess had sent out for reinforcements.

"We just want to see the show," said Sully. "We've got plenty of money."

The bouncer (What else could he be? He was even bigger than the Slime People.) handed Sully his wallet.

"Be reasonable, boys," he said. "At least try to look twenty-one."

Sully and I inspected one another. Jeans and T-shirts. Mine said BRADLEYVILLE P.E.

"Now," he said, "I've probably got a guy or two in here tonight who's a little less than legal, okay? But he made the effort; he put on a suit and tie. If the cops come in, they nose around and at least everything looks kosher. If I let you guys in and they see you in your diapers, they got no choice. They have to lift my license. Understand?"

"Yes, sir," we said in unison.

"Good. So no hard feelings." He pointed to me. "This one's not driving, is he?"

"No, sir."

"Also good. Now, you remember where the door is?" His hand on my shoulder weighed about nine pounds.

Outside I leaned on the nearest car. "I don't care, Sully. I'm going to tell her anyway."

"Think it over. See how you feel in the morning."

"Do you think she'll hate me?"

"Don't be dumb. Just think it over, that's all."

I could hear the music build, and the sound of the crowd.

"It was pretty grungy, wasn't it?"

"It's just a place, Walker," he said, trying to sound convincing. "And anyway, Rachel loves you."

"What would you do?"

"I don't know," he said quickly. "C'mon."

"But you're the doctor. You always know."

"I know you shouldn't drink any more wine."

I put my hand to my stomach. "All of a sudden," I said, "I don't feel so good."

"Walker?" My mom's voice was so faint I thought it was part of my dreams. "Honey, are you okay?"

I rolled over, then waited while the room — like the bubble in a carpenter's level — evened out.

Tap, tap, tap. "Walker?"

"Coming, yes." I groped for my old Scooby-Doo bathrobe, then opened the door. "What time is it?"

"Almost noon. I got your note."

"My note."

Mom followed me down the hall. "The one I translated into 'Let me sleep.'"

"Oh, yeah," I said, pausing at the bathroom door. "That note." What note? I didn't remember writing any note.

"Will you come into the kitchen when you're finished?"

The light above the sink was awful, a flashbulb that never stopped. I looked at myself in the mirror, then turned away, quicker than a vampire. I was so woozy that I sat down to pee, grateful that Sully wasn't around to bring up John Wayne again, his father's hero. Finally I brushed my teeth and my tongue, pushed my hair around a little, and went into the kitchen.

"I won't kiss you," my mother said, "if you have the flu. Exotic dancers have a lot of strange gimmicks, but throwing up on the front tables isn't one of them."

"I don't have the flu," I said, looking her right in the eye. "I got drunk with Sully."

"I figured. You smell like a drunk. Want some eggs?"

"I may never eat again."

As I sat down at the table, Mom reached for my hand and patted it.

"I remember my first hangover," she said. "Yuck. But you'll feel better soon." Then she asked seriously, "You didn't drive, did you?"

I shook my head. "Sully did. But he wasn't drinking."

"Okay, but take it easy with that stuff, all right?"

I nodded, a little ashamed of myself. "Oh, did Rachel call?"

"No, but her father did. I keep telling him to talk to you, but he doesn't seem to get it."

"Does he want to buy the place lock, stock, and oats?"

"There's been some kind of hitch. He sounded peeved. I think it's going to come down to an option to buy."

I shook my head to show I didn't know what that was.

"Sort of a dog-in-the-manger deal. While he has the option to buy, nobody else can, but it doesn't mean he will."

"But I get paid?"

"Enough to get you started in college, anyway."

"Mr. Kramer said once that we might lease what I've got for grazing, and if Rachel's dad didn't care, maybe we could put in a cash crop next year."

"Do you think so? Every little bit would help."

Talking so earnestly had just about worn me out. "I think I need a little more sleep," I said, managing a half smile. I got up, then sat right back down again. "I'm sorry I got drunk last night. I won't do it again. Honest."

She smiled at me. "You're a great kid, you know that? I hear women complain about their children all the time. Then I tell them about you."

Embarrassed, I started to get up; instead, though, I

212

took both her hands, made them into a fist, covered that with mine. "I went to the club. Sully and I did."

"Really? What'd you think?" She seemed genuinely interested.

"I didn't see much. We couldn't get past the girl at the door."

"But you got the general idea."

"Why do you do it? Why do you work there?"

"Do you think if I really loved you I wouldn't? Is it like a test I have to pass?" She wasn't angry. Her voice was soft.

I shook my head. "No, not really. It's just such a wretched place."

She smiled, extracted two or three fingers from under mine, and rubbed the back of my hands. "Wretched, huh? I guess it did look that way last night. We had something like six soccer teams from Kansas City. All the losers. So you can imagine the mood they were in." She sat back reflectively. "They were crude and they tipped like Scrooge."

"So if it's so bad . . ." I persisted.

"You know, sweetheart, lots of times it's not. The pay is good, it's fun sometimes, and I always like to be forty and still able to get up there and hold their attention."

"It all seems so hard. Your job, I mean." I felt shaky inside. "Much harder than I ever imagined."

"Why is that?"

"You know when Sully and I were standing there trying to get in?"

"Uh-huh." She smiled encouragingly.

"I saw part of somebody's act."

She leaned toward me again, combing back my hair, the same color as hers.

"And I guess I want to know if you have to do that, too."

"Do what, sweetheart?"

"Climb the curtain every night."

I could see the question mark in her eyes. Then she began to laugh, hands on her knees, head back, roaring like a drunken lord. She looked great. Light was almost shooting off of her. I hadn't heard her laugh like that since before Dad died.

"So you cried while you were talking to your mom?" Sully asked as I untaped the tractor picture from the inside of my locker.

"Yeah, a little."

"God, that's great. I think my parents would take my car away if I cried. My dad thinks tears cause cancer." Sully shook his head in disbelief, then asked, "Did you tell your mom that you were going to tell Rachel?"

I shook my head.

"But you are."

I nodded.

"Is today the day?"

"Yesterday was the day, but Rachel wasn't at school."

"Is she okay?" he asked.

"I saw her car in the lot this morning."

"Look, I'm sure everything will be fine."

"Thank you, doctor."

"My bill is in the mail." Then Sully was off to class.

I didn't feel like telling him I was having second and third thoughts. I knew what I hoped Rachel would say, but I also knew she might say anything. She never mentioned her mother's name without lowering her voice reverently, and there was mine up there, shaking it for all the second-rate soccer players in the world.

Or I guess she shook it. I didn't really know. And didn't really want to know. Rachel would just have to make do without documentation.

I had, though, gone to the reference shelf for help: *Stripper*, for instance, really seemed crude — drums, bumps, grinds, long black gloves tossed out into the seething crowd. *Dancer* wasn't entirely honest, was it? I mean, ballerinas were dancers. *Ecdysiast* was interesting: it would just make mom sound woozy, but then Rachel would ask what it meant and I'd be back to square one.

Entertainer? Artiste? Performer? Chorus girl? Danseuse? My God, she would think I'd eaten a thesaurus.

Nothing would do but the truth. And what was that? She wasn't a bartender or a waitress. She worked at a club called Ye Olde Burlesque and she was a dancer. Take it or leave it.

Then I spotted Rachel trudging down the hall toward me. I waved both hands; she blinked in acknowledgment. I was like a flag; she was like a penlight.

"Hi" I said eagerly. "Hi."

"Hi," she said without looking up. Her backpack dangled off one shoulder. She shifted until it hung between us.

"There's something I want to tell you," I began, "something I should have told you a long time ago."

Rachel sighed and looked at her shoes. Jesus, did she know already?

"What's wrong?" I asked.

"Nothing."

"Sure there is."

"Then why ask if you already know?"

"I don't know what, I just know —"

"I have to go to class."

My stomach felt like a cold, wet sock.

"Are you sick?"

"I don't know, maybe."

216

Her voice was absolutely flat. It all reminded me of *Invasion of the Body Snatchers*. Had a pod grown over-night into this lifeless copy?

"Did you eat breakfast?"

She shook her head and began to drift away.

"Wait." I started to dig in my bookbag. "This has a lot of potassium."

"Let me get this straight," said Sully as we stood in the parking lot after school. "She threw your banana at you?"

"Hit me right in the face." I pointed to a nick on my cheekbone.

"Forever scarred by a tropical fruit."

"Screw you — it hurt."

"And you didn't get to tell her, so that wasn't it."

"I think she knows, otherwise why . . . ?"

Sully shook his head. "Not likely. I think she would have just come out with it. No, it's something else."

"You should see the pictures of her mom: flowers, incense, it's like a shrine out there."

"How did she act again?"

"Listless. Pissed off. Surly."

"Four more and we have all seven dwarfs."

"Are you being a shithead on purpose, or is this your idea of concern?"

"Sorry. I just can't take it seriously. Probably she

flunked a test or argued with her dad or started her period. This can't last."

"Honest?"

"Trust me. I'm a trained observer of human nature."

Mom was back on her regular schedule, but I still had enough time to drive out to my field for an hour or two. There'd been another thunderstorm, but the heavy rain hadn't hurt anything. The stalks were completely resilient, getting back up again on their own as soon as the sun was out.

As I walked up and down the rows, stooping every now and then to wipe out a weed or to repair some tiny earthen dam, I think part of me envied the oats.

Whoever heard of a grain being depressed or lovelorn? They just grew up, pollinated one another, and that was that. But there were no ecstatic oats, either. No oat who dreamed of another oat like I did of Rachel.

I decided to hope that Sully was right.

But the next day was, if anything, worse. I found her leaning against the wall beside her locker like a sick animal. I knocked softly on the green metal door. When she looked up at me, her chin began to quiver.

"I called you last night."

"I know," she whispered.

I reached for her, then took my hand back. "Rachel, what's wrong?"

She shook her head.

"Don't tell me 'Nothing.' I'm not nuts, you know."

"I didn't say you were." I could barely hear her.

"Then tell me."

She slammed the heel of her right hand against her forehead, ground it down until it obliterated one eye, and finally choked out five words. "I have to move again."

"Move? Move where?"

She shook her head.

"When?"

"My dad's so mad."

"At you? For what?"

"Bradleyville. They won't rezone for him. He can't build the Garden."

"I thought you were never going to move again. I thought he said —"

"He did," she cried. "He promised a hundred times. Then all of a sudden he says he's changed his mind." She snapped her fingers soundlessly. "Just like that."

"Don't go."

"I have to."

"No, you don't. Peggy didn't. Her folks are God knows where. You could —"

"I'm not Peggy. I'm not anything like Peggy." People in the hall turned to stare. "I love my father. We've been together since my mom died. We're all we've got."

That was Tuesday of the second or third grimmest week of my life. Wednesday was different, but no better. It was just my turn to lean against the lockers and to drag myself up and down the halls like I was pulling a barge. And it was Rachel's turn to come up to me.

"I'm sorry about yesterday, Walker."

She was dressed completely in white: a snow goddess. And cold like you wouldn't believe. Even her breath felt cold.

"This is a painful situation for both of us, but there's no reason we still can't be friends." Her eyes were blank; she was reading off some frozen tablet in her head. "Naturally we'll want to see other people."

"You're nuts, Rachel. I don't want to see other people, and I don't think you do either."

It seemed to shake her a little, but only a little. "We might date, then, on a casual basis, naturally: movies, concerts . . ."

I slammed the locker door. "Cut it out — now. I mean it."

"I see," she said, and her voice broke, "that you aren't mature enough to —"

"I love you, Rachel, but I couldn't tell you or wouldn't or just didn't know how, but now —"

"Don't, Walker, please . . ." The whole icy facade collapsed. "Don't" she moaned. "I can't . . ."

I put my arms around her, and for a second it was like it had been when we were alone saying good night or under Kramer's oak and our skin just seemed to dissolve and our cells and our blood ran together and we weren't two people anymore, just one.

"Then?" asked Sully.

"You know that story in the Bible about Lot's wife, who turns into a pillar of salt? Well, she was a noodle compared to Rachel."

"She pushed you away?"

"Went stiff as a board." I shifted the phone to my other ear. "What would you do if you were me?"

"Look, I'm supposed to pick up Peggy in a few minutes. Let's all go get something to eat, and we'll talk."

"I'm not hungry."

"God, this *is* serious."

"Well, maybe I could eat a piece of butter lettuce."

When I got in the car, Peggy patted my hand consolingly, but nobody said much on our way to the brand-new, retro A&W. Sully liked the A&W better than any other fast-food place in town because it had hamburgers named after the family unit — Juniorburger, Mommaburger, and Daddy-burger — and the Freudian overtones amused him. The four of us — Rachel and Peggy, Sully and I — had laughed ourselves sick one night setting up housekeeping with our snacks, including the foreign neighbors, the Fry family from France. I guess it sounds stupid when I write it down, but it was funny that night and thinking about it again just made me feel so thick and heavy it was like I was wearing lead underwear.

"I don't want anything," I said to the carhop.

"At least have a double Mommaburger," Sully urged.

"Forget that. I can't handle the one mother I've got."

Sully ordered something for me and rolled up the window. Then he and Peggy turned to stare, both their chins resting on the spotless leather.

"How about not looking at me like I'm the last California condor, okay?"

"Sorry," Peggy said. "You just seem so miserable."

"Well, I am miserable."

"She's miserable, too."

"How do you know that?"

"Walker, I talk to her every night on the phone."

"Really?"

"Really. And you should tell her how you feel."

"Well, I feel terrible."

"You should tell her," said Sully.

"I just miss her so much."

"You should tell her," Peggy urged.

"I sleep crappy."

"Tell her," they said in unison.

"And I think about her all the time."

"Tell her," they chanted.

"Even when I make a sandwich and I put on the bologna and the salami and the Braunschweiger, when I get to the part with the tomato I always see her little face right there on top."

Sully and Peggy looked at each other. "Don't tell her that," they said.

Just then the carhop skated back and Sully handed out the food. He had ordered me a plain Juniorburger. I took off the sesame part of the bun, furtively wrote my name in ketchup and Rachel's in mustard, then pressed the halves together tenderly.

"Eat," said Peggy. "C'mon."

I took a little bite. "God, I worry about her. I wonder if she's okay, I wonder if she's eating right, I wonder what she's doing." I put my hamburger back into its carton decorated with happy couples dining with both hands. "What if she starts going out with somebody else and likes it?"

"She won't," Peggy said. "We talked about that.

She's not like I used to be: break up with one on Friday and get three new ones by Saturday."

Sully pitched forward into the steering wheel, wheezing and coughing. Peggy slapped him on the back until part of a French fry flew out and stuck to the speedometer.

"Nice shot," she said. "Right at fifty-five. Just never go faster than that potato and you'll be safe."

"You know," I said thoughtfully, "when Debbie moved away, I felt like this, but part of me was relieved, too. Isn't that funny?"

"Why were you relieved?" asked Sully, nibbling carefully.

"I'm not sure. I liked Debbie. I sure liked kissing her. I didn't want that part to ever stop."

Peggy smiled at me over the back of her seat as her hand slipped over toward Sully's.

"But honestly," she said, "how much fun would it be if it didn't? It'd be like being in tenth grade forever."

"Look, what would you do about Rachel?"

She frowned as she thought. "Rachel's a real girl," she said deliberately. "I mean she cooks for her dad and takes care of his clothes and all that."

"Right. So?"

"Well, you might have to get on your horse and go get her."

"Now?"

"Finish your Juniorburger," she said, trying to keep it light.

But she turned to Sully. "You tell him, Sully. You know more about this psychology stuff than I do."

"No, I don't," he said evenly. "I've just read a lot of stupid books. You're a hundred times smarter than I am."

"God, Sully." Peggy put one hand to her lips like she might cry. "That's the nicest thing you ever said to me."

"I'm going to miss you so much in September."

"Jeez, me too." Peggy suddenly sounded all broken up.

"I already miss Rachel," I whined from the back seat.

Our hamburgers rose in unison and bumped into our quivering lips. We stared at each over the droopy buns.

Then the corner of Peggy's mouth started to twitch, Sully's eyes brightened, and we all started to laugh.

That was the best I'd felt in days.

Monday, though, school was just another trip to the Planet of Misery. And work was no better. Everywhere out there reminded me of Rachel — where we had eaten lunch or made love or taken a nap or talked about what we would do the next day, the next week and month, the next year.

Then on the second Saturday night after we'd broken

up, I just picked up the phone, called Rachel — and got nothing. Not even the machine. Casually I hung up. Casually I went into the bathroom and turned on the hot water.

Self-deception is funny. Part of me was just soaking in the tub; part of me knew I was about to set out on a quest. Part of me was still very casual — shaving, checking myself out in the mirror, smoothing on after-shave; part of me was hurrying the razor, rejecting that shirt and those pants, slapping on the after-shave hard enough to snap the average person out of a little fit of hysteria.

I had the car because that guy Porter — who'd turned into pretty much of a steady boyfriend, I guess — had picked Mom up. Driving toward Rachel's — still casual, right? One arm out the window, the side vent arranged so the wind would hopefully blow my hair with wild abandon instead of right in my eyes — carfuls of girls checked me out, giggling, waving, doing mysterious, semaphore things with their eyes.

Isn't it funny? That's what I'd always wanted: girls who were interested in me as me and not just some chubby kid who would give them directions to the nearest Snack Shack. And then I got what I wanted, and it didn't mean a thing. Not that I wasn't flattered or even, let's face it, a little interested. But it didn't really matter.

Isn't that amazing? If I live to be a hundred, there are some things I'm never going to understand.

Of course Rachel wasn't home. Even the garage was empty, but that didn't mean anything. She and her dad took separate cars to dinner all the time so she could leave while he wooed prospective clients with tales of paradise.

Since there was a good chance she was at Peggy's, I headed that way, but nobody was home there, either. Or at Sully's.

Okay, maybe she wasn't alone. Maybe she was "seeing other people" for a hamburger, a trip around the skating rink, or a movie at the drive-in. Big deal. Very innocent.

At the Moonlight Rollerdrome I strolled in, waved to some people, leaned across the barrier, and scoped the place out. She could be holding hands with somebody while she skated. For safety's sake. He could even have his arm around her waist. That's how it was done on skates. It didn't have to mean anything.

"Seen Rachel?" I asked a couple of girls skating backward, but they shook their heads.

At the A&W I resisted ordering absolutely everything and, when she wasn't there and hadn't been there, headed for Big Sky Drive-in.

"Seen Rachel?" I asked a guy I knew at the admission booth.

"Not yet, but I just came on."

"Seen Rachel?" I asked some kids at the refreshment stand. "Seen Rachel?" I asked, standing outside under the moth-filled funnel of light from the projector.

Always the same answer: No, nope, uh-uh, not lately, not tonight. Then as I made one last sweep of the place, I spotted what could have been her in a Firebird with California plates. Had an old boyfriend shown up from the West Coast? They were outlined — the two of them — against the enormous screen, nose to nose, pucker to pucker like a Valentine silhouette. I studied them through the back window while I wondered what to do.

Now that it's over, I can think of a dozen other plans, all of them better: I might have taken the flashlight out of the trunk and pretended to be an employee, or simply bought a box of popcorn and got close enough by merely acting lost.

Instead, I parked a couple of rows ahead of them, slithered out of the passenger's side, and crept up to the Firebird's grill on all fours. Then, like some dark moon rising, my head slowly emerged from behind the hood ornament.

Naturally the girl shrieked. Who could blame her?

She was watching *Aliens from Zoron* and here comes this thing out of the front of the car.

But it wasn't Rachel's shriek, and by the time the guy even got the speaker off his window, I was back in the trusty Saturn, throwing gravel and heading west. Because it'd dawned on me where Rachel had gone. Where did she always go? Where, for that matter, did most kids go?

"Seen Rachel?" I asked the first bunch of girls I saw at Westgate, all of them dressed alike, all with their hair done the same, all angling left then right in unison like a school of pretty fish.

"Just Desserts," they said.

Great! But what would I do when I found her, pretend I was just there for a triple-dip rocky road?

Carefully, wearing an imaginary trench coat and Bogart hat, I peered around the edge of the window plastered with gaudy sweets. No Rachel. I didn't know whether to be relieved or disappointed.

"Looking for Rachel?" someone said behind me, and I jumped.

"Jesus, Billy." It was a guy from English Lit.

"She just came out of Nordstrom."

"Thanks." I broke into an easy canter.

"Seen Rachel?" I asked right outside the department store doors.

"Try the lower level."

With a groan I plunged down the stairs, bumping people, excusing myself, not excusing myself, emerging to see her with Tommy Thompson's loathsome arm draped across her shoulder.

If I'd had a gun, I would have shot him in the foot; if I'd had a club, I would have beaned him. As it was, I ran up and bit him in the wrist.

"Jesus," he cried whirling around, shaking his hand like it was burned. "What's the matter with you?"

Rachel turned, her face knotted in disbelief.

"You're not Rachel," I said happily.

"Who's Rachel?" she turned on Tommy. "Who's this Rachel?"

"I'll have to get rabies shots," he said, inspecting his wrist.

"I'm sorry, honest." I began to back away. "I'm really sorry. Really." Then I turned and ran.

Upstairs, I went into the men's room, hardly recognizing myself in the mirror. My hair was plastered to my skull, I was flushed, and somehow my shirt had been twisted so that one sleeve was very short and the other very long. When I bent to wash my face, I got one cuff completely soaked. And if that wasn't bad enough, I smelled. It was the worst kind of perspiration, the stuff that sets off alarms on TV or leaves people flattened in its wake.

Good Lord, if Rachel did see me, she wouldn't recognize me. If she recognized me, she would shriek and run; if she didn't run and for some reason put her arms around me, I'd feel and smell like an old washrag.

"Forget it," I said, pushing open the bathroom door. And then, naturally, there she was not twenty feet away, staring into the window of Tom's Travels. Startled, I darted into the nearest store, peering out at her from between the mannequins in the window.

"May I help you?"

"Oh, uh, sure," I said to the saleslady, whose purple hair reminded me of Mom's violets. I reached into the nearest bin. "This," I said. "It's a gift."

"You're sure?" she said suspiciously.

Outside Rachel drifted away. "Absolutely. Wrap it up."

"This is a panty girdle for the full-figured woman." And she held it up with both hands.

It was the color of Petunia Pig and about as large. "Oh, well," I said. "Full-figured. Well." If I wasn't hemming and hawing, I was at least hemming. Backing away, I bumped into another counter, reached behind me, plunged one hand into another bin. "These, then. Instead."

"And what would those be?" she asked, starting to lose her patience.

I looked at them. "Uh, I don't know."

"Panties," she said.

"You're kidding." I looked again. Panties were what Rachel wore, little dainty things as pretty and fragile as flowers. These were industrial strength. The elastic could have shot me across the room. I dropped them like they were hot.

"I think I'd better call security."

"No, no," I assured her. "Honest, I'm leaving. It's a mistake. It's all a terrible mistake."

I retreated to the parking lot. Like in those old Greek plays, the madness had passed and I was purged. As I sat on the fender idly looking one way and then the other, I didn't even worry about which side was my good side or even if, like a record that never sold, I had two bad ones.

Then as the crowds thinned, as the security men ushered the late shoppers out and locked the gates to the Magic Kingdom of Things, there she was. Alone.

She didn't see me; she was walking with her head down, scuffing one shoe on the asphalt like a little kid.

I watched her stop, hesitate, run one hand roughly through her hair, then turn, stride to the nearest waste can, and drop in the bag she'd been carrying. Finally she whirled and strode resolutely toward her car. Until she saw me.

I raised one hand tentatively, a mini-wave. Less than that, a micro-wave. She nodded in reply. And even though it was shadowy in the huge lot I was sure I saw her smile.

Then she started toward me. Flustered, I sat down again, goosing myself on the hood ornament, but I think she was still too far away to see me wince.

When we were a few yards apart, she stopped. I smiled encouragingly. She raised both hands tentatively, then sort of kept raising them and hugged herself.

"Walker," she said softly. "I'm so glad to see you."

"I, uh, called you a couple of hours ago and when you weren't home I started to look for you."

"Well, here I am," she said holding out both arms like someone showing off a new dress.

"Yeah, me too. I'm here too." I stood up, kind of patting myself to show I wasn't an apparition.

We looked at one another, half grinning, half embarrassed.

"How've you been?" she asked.

I shrugged. "You know."

She glanced down at her hands, one curled palm up in the other, like a soloist's.

"I miss you, Rachel."

She started to look teary. "I was just in the mall missing you."

"Me too."

"Isn't that dumb? We should have just got together and missed each other."

Little by little we were getting closer, she moving warily in one direction, I in the other. I'd seen a movie in biology like this, but it was about a couple of birds.

"You know what my dad wants to do now?"

"Build the first mall on the moon?"

"Stay in Bradleyville."

That stopped me in my tracks. "You're kidding."

"Oh, who knows with him?"

"But he said it."

"Sure, but I've been so miserable, it was probably just to make me feel better."

"Well, it makes me feel better."

"Me too, but I'm afraid he'll change his mind again."

I shrugged. "But until he does . . ."

Involuntarily we started toward each other again. I knew how it was going to feel to kiss Rachel and to hold her warm, sturdy body. I was just about to open my arms as wide as they would go and scoop her up when I remembered. And stopped dead in my tracks.

"Wait a minute," I said. "There's something else."

"What? Are you mad? I don't blame you. I should apologize. . . ."

I shook my head. "Something about me."

"About you? Walker, what?" She looked really concerned. "It doesn't matter, whatever it is. You're okay, aren't you?"

"My mom . . ." I said cryptically.

"Is she hurt?"

". . . is a stripper," I said, a lot louder than necessary. "She's a dancer, but she dances at some place called Ye Olde Burlesque, probably with her clothes off. So . . ." I looked away, then down at her feet. My eyes swept the ground like someone who has lost a key. "So if you don't want to be around somebody whose mom —"

"Walker," she said softly, "I know all that."

I fell back against the car. "You do?"

"I found out a few weeks ago. Tommy Thompson asked me how I like going out with somebody whose mom was a topless dancer. I just told him to stuff it."

"You don't care?" I couldn't believe it.

"Your mom's nice. God, my dad bullies people until they sell him their homes. What's worse?"

"But didn't you wonder why I'd never said anything? What about all those lies about her being a waitress and all?"

"I thought you'd tell me sooner or later. Anyway," she said sweetly, "everybody's got secrets."

"But if you know and Sully and Peggy know, then lots of people know."

"Probably almost everybody."

"How come nobody ever said anything to me before?"

She shrugged. "So they'll kid you tomorrow."

They'd kid me. They'd kid me tomorrow. And that's what it would amount to — kidding. All this time and nobody really cared but me.

I loved holding Rachel in my arms again, and we just leaned against my fender for a few minutes until our breathing slowed and meshed.

Around us the other isolated cars crept away. Nearby a shiny Porsche pulled up beside a Chevy minivan whose interior was lined with baby seats. The couple in the Porsche embraced; then a woman slipped out, glanced around furtively, and fumbled — alone and in the dark — with her car keys.

Maybe Rachel had been right all along and the mall was the new community. Certainly everything happened here. Tonight lovers used the parking lot instead of a side street or park bench. Last week a woman had gone into labor right in Pet's Delight.

"Where were you born?" someone would ask that child, and he would answer, "In the mall." "Where have you been?" the anxious husband would ask. "At the mall." If things kept going like this, my mother would end up dancing at the food court.

"My God," I said, stepping back. "Do you know what we should do?"

"Yes, start kissing and never stop."

"No. I mean yes, but no. We should go and see my mother."

"Where is she, home?"

I shook my head. "Working. At the club. Dancing." I was talking like a faucet, going on and off. "We could see her. See what she really does. Sort of. Maybe wave to her. Or something."

"You go," she said softly but firmly. "I need to see my father."

"No. I mean, sure, but why? What's he doing?"

"Probably waiting for dinner right now, banging his spoon on his dish."

"Afterward, then. You could dress up and look twenty-one easy."

"You go, sweetheart." She touched my chest lightly, not off to the left where everybody pledges allegiance, but almost in the center, where the heart really is.

"I just don't want to go alone, do I?"

"I don't want to face my dad, either. But I was thinking about a lot of things in the mall tonight, and I just

don't want to be his bookkeeper anymore. Or cook breakfast for him every morning or tell the cleaners there's a
spot on his cashmere sweater."

"What's he going to do?"

She shrugged and smiled. "What *can* he do, threaten
to move?"

I drove home and paged through the closet until I found
my only suit, the one I hadn't worn since my father's
funeral. Peggy had cut my hair so that it stuck up styl-
ishly, but I slicked it back and even tried to part it on the
side like an adult. Or, anyway, like my idea of an adult.
Okay, okay — the truth: like my father.

When the phone rang, it was Rachel. "Are you okay?"

"I got my pants on with the zipper in front — that's
a step in the right direction. How about you?"

"Dad's on the other phone downstairs. Probably buying Asia. Call me when you get back, please."

"Really? This could take a while."

"For me, too. This is going to push all my father's buttons. Call me on my phone, okay? We'll talk about what we
want to do tomorrow. I want to see the oats. I miss them."

"They miss you. Every time I went out there, they
asked about you."

"Well, I think I hear the heavy tread of the professional parent."

"Yeah, and I think I hear the music all the way from Love's Park."

A different blonde reading a paperback as big as a brick hardly looked up as I came in.

"Table or the bar?" she asked, holding out her hand for the admission.

The bar was farther away from the stage, so I chose that, slipping in beside a man with arms so hairy I thought he was wearing a sweater. In front of him were half a dozen tiny umbrellas, carefully folded. Another, opened, decorated his tall tropical drink.

"What'll it be?" asked the bartender. "Three-drink minimum, you get 'em all now. When the show starts, I go on break."

Everyone had glasses in front of him. A bald man had one in each hand, holding on like they were levers. Another guy arranged his into an arrowhead; a third made a long, even line; and a fourth filled his with ashes and bent filters.

If Sully had been there, he could have done a psychological profile on each one: heavy-equipment operator, cowboy, drill sergeant, slob.

"Uh, do you have a Diet Coke?"

"Three Diet Cokes comin' up."

A very tinny combo hidden behind sequined curtains

at the far edge of the stage swung into "How High the Moon." My father only owned a dozen albums; four of them were by Les Paul and Mary Ford; out of all the songs on all the albums, "How High the Moon" had been his favorite. I wondered if Mom was backstage listening and, if so, what was she thinking about?

Casually I turned to inspect the room. There were lots of women with their boyfriends or husbands, though why women would want to see other women take their clothes off was beyond me.

I was surprised at how well behaved everybody was; people chatted over their drinks, laughed those sound-less laughs, and waited patiently, tapping an index finger in time to the music.

My worst fears were that the winners of some play-offs would show up, teams with names like the Drooling Cretins. And there were a few tables of rough-looking guys, but mostly the same kind of people you'd see in a doctor's office, just more of them.

Ta-daah! The master of ceremonies was good-looking, if you like those marinated types, and he wore gold chains with links almost as big as the ones we used on our tires in the winter.

The show opened with a comedy sketch. There was a judge, a peeping Tom, and a French maid. I think it's probably enough to say that the main joke was the misunderstanding between "Your Honor" and "You're on her."

Still, people laughed. The judge hit the peeping Tom with his gavel; the maid clutched her rouged cheeks in mock terror. I just got more and more nervous.

"And now," boomed the MC, "here she is, wearing only beads . . . of perspiration — Wanda, the Wildcat of Burlesque."

Wanda may have been onstage for ten minutes, and she was never one mile per hour below top speed. Those in front leaned back, and a few shielded their eyes like they were watching a fire. She sped around the stage with her teeth bared; she threw herself on a bear rug so hard that I was afraid she had broken something; and for a finale Wanda climbed the main curtain again, screaming all the time and slamming her pelvis into the air. She'd exploded onstage wearing very little to begin with — just a sort of hairy bra and panties — and this time she didn't take off a stitch. When we applauded at the end, we applauded like physicists celebrating pure energy.

A tenor was next, piping to a stunned house about Ireland and mothers; then a skit with two beds, three doors, and four newlyweds.

Monique, direct from the Côte d'Azur, glided around

the stage dragging a fur for what seemed like hours; then — as if to show us she had other skills — she twirled the tassels on her breasts clockwise and counterclockwise. Monique was a big woman, anyway, and with her arms straight out and her tassels going, she looked like a World War II bomber waiting for takeoff. To finish, she urged the crowd to count over the drum roll as she tried for three hundred, a personal best. Something went wrong in the two hundreds, but we gave her a hand anyway.

Then it was time. "Her name's Virginia," said old oil-and-chains, "but she's no virgin."

I turned on my stool and hung my head, like a kid in class who doesn't know the answer.

"And she came to us via Las Vegas from Gay Paree. Let's have a big hand for the cleanest act in burlesque — the Virgin Queen, Virginia LaRue."

So far all the dancers except Wanda had been from France; according to this guy, there was nobody in France but strippers, all standing at the coast in their high heels and feather boas waiting for the next boat to Kansas City.

The music was playing; the lights were down; the spot was on. Everybody was watching but me. I just stared at the ceiling.

"Nice," said the man next to me, so I sneaked a look.

My mother sat in a bogus bedroom with her back to the audience, jauntily slipping off leg warmers, headband, and sweatshirt.

When she stood up from the flimsy vanity table and turned around, there was her K.C. Royals T-shirt, which drew some scattered applause from the sportsmen in the crowd.

I was fascinated and appalled. I struggled to look at the stage. Involuntarily my hands leaped up and clamped themselves over my eyes. All I could hear were the shouts and whistles; all I could feel was the place coming alive.

I peeked out from between my fingers; my heart was beating like crazy and I was short of breath. I could just see the headline — STRIPPER'S SON DIES AT LATE SHOW.

Then she slipped off her T-shirt, holding it against her coyly. Someone actually shouted, "C'mon, honey. Take it all off." I wanted to storm over there and ask how *he* would like it if somebody talked about *his* mother that way.

Suddenly the lights went down, the music slowed, and out of the wings came half a plastic globe seething with soapsuds.

So that was her gimmick. No snakes, hula hoops, or tassels, but a tub: the cleanest act in show business. I put my head in my hands. Oh, my God, oh, my God. Taking a bath in front of a hundred strangers. Her legs emerged from the foam and her fingers tiptoed down them.

"I hope her bubble bath is like what my wife buys at Thrifty's," my neighbor said. "It goes flat in about two seconds."

I guess I was about to faint, because I remember feeling flushed and lightheaded. Then I had the weirdest experience. I've never told it to anybody, even Sully, up until now.

What happened was that all of a sudden it was like I could see everything from the upper left-hand corner of the room. There I was, my face nearly on the bar from embarrassment. There was everybody else — all the bald heads, all the perms and sets, all the good clothes and the bad. I could see the band, professionally bored; I could see the bartender idly wiping a glass, and I could see a waitress sitting near the jukebox rubbing her feet.

And I felt such tenderness for everybody who had brought his mortality out of the house and into this silly club. I knew that I was suffering needlessly. I looked at my mother, half buried in suds, and I loved her so much; but then I loved the bartender, too, and the woman with the artificial pearls, and her husband with the worst hairpiece in the world; I loved the thugs with their scruffy beards and the waitress whose feet I could have kissed. I saw my hands fall away from my eyes. I saw myself smile and applaud.

Then, just like I had evaporated through the ceiling, I was outside, hovering above the broken shingles, just to one side of my car parked by the side door.

Slowly I floated upward. There was Kansas City and the land I had worked on; beyond was the Mississippi, dividing the republic; there were the Great Plains, the Rockies, the two oceans sloping toward the east and west just like the blue globe at school.

Then there was the earth itself, resting in space; and I knew if I wanted to, I could open my arms and somehow embrace everything: all the weirdness and folly and beauty and bliss.

So I did. I opened my arms and the earth came rushing at me, eager as a pup.

"She's great," someone shouted, getting to his feet to applaud. "God, she's great."

Mom came out of the wings wrapped in a plushy towel, and took a few bows. She looked terrific: flushed and happy. She opened her arms just like I'd done, welcoming it all; then giving it back, blowing kisses everywhere.

Then it was over. Everyone sat down, pleased and exhilarated. The MC urged us to wait through the intermission. There was a triple finale, three dancers from France.

"Excuse me," I said to the blond cashier, who was, unbelievably, nearly finished with her book. "I'd like to see Virginia LaRue."

"You and twenty other guys."

"It's not like that," I assured her. "I'm her son." I smiled proudly.

"You're kidding."

"No."

"She said she had a kid. So you're the farmer."

"Just forty acres. It's not like —"

"I was brought up on a farm. I hated it. I could never keep my shoes clean."

She swung one silver pump out from behind the counter. I tried to picture her anywhere but Ye Olde Burlesque and failed.

"So could I see my mom?"

"Sure, cutie. But go around the side, okay?"

I guess I half expected a crusty old watchman in suspenders to ask me what I wanted, but there was nobody inside the back door at all, just a water cooler, a small bathroom, and of all things, a bowling ball inside an alligator bag. Which one, I wondered, tassels packed away safely for the night, relaxed with a cold beer at the nearest alley?

Down the narrow hall was a half-open door, and when I knocked, it swung open. A woman dressed in three leaves was hauling her boa constrictor out of its box.

"Whadayawant?" she asked, beginning to wipe the snake down with a paper towel.

"To see Virginia if I can, Virginia LaRue."

"Yeah? Who shall I say is calling, Matt Damon?"

"Just say a fan."

She didn't go "Harumph," but she looked it. "Hey, Virginia, there's some kid here who looks like an undertaker's apprentice."

I heard chairs shift and squeak, a muttered "Watch it," and then, "Walker?" She reached for the top buttons of her robe. "What are you doing here?"

I leaned in the doorway. "Seeing the show. I thought it'd be a shame to never see you dance."

"Well." She looked around helplessly. "Well. I don't know what to say."

"You were pretty good. Really."

"Thanks." She began to blush. "I mean it, thanks." She gestured behind her, a modified umpire's *Yer out!* "Listen, come in for a minute. I want you to meet everybody."

It was probably a cruddy little room with peeling paint and no toilet, but the prospect of half a dozen women with most of their clothes off seemed like heaven to me.

"Listen up," she said, tapping on a steam pipe with a nail polish bottle. "This is my son."

Most of them gave me the once-over, then returned

to their toes or nails or eyes or whatever part of their bodies they were polishing.

"Uh, this is Eve," Mom said, pointing to the woman with the snake. "I mean it's Doris, but —"

"Whoever heard of Adam and Doris?" She squinted at me through her cigarette smoke.

"Yes, ma'am."

I nodded or said hello to everyone, even Wanda, who was sitting in a corner with a ball of yarn in her lap.

"If she knits as fast as she dances," I said, "we're all liable to be swallowed up in a sweater."

Wanda didn't laugh, but Mom did. She put her hand up to my forehead like she was checking for fever, then let it slide down to my cheek in a caress.

"I'm very glad to see you, Walker."

"Hi." It was a man's voice and it came from behind me.

"Oh, hi." Mom got a little flustered as Porter squeezed past. "You remember —"

"Walker, sure. Hi. You saw the show?"

"Yeah, I uh . . ."

"Got in and everything?"

Eve put some of her snake in my hands. "Hold this for a minute, will ya, kid?"

"Look," Porter began, "we were going . . ."

But my mom began, too, "Look, we were . . ."

They both laughed; Mom put her arm around his

waist. That got me a little. I'd never seen her do that except with Dad, and then only when they were having their picture taken.

I handed my part of the snake to Porter. "I better get home," I said.

"We were going out to eat," he said. "Come along."

"No, really." I started to back away.

"Pizza," he said seductively, holding out about a yard of boa constrictor.

"Thanks," I said, waving from the safety of the hall. "Really, thanks."

Outside I leaned my forehead against the cool plastic of the steering wheel. Just then Mom tapped on the window and I rolled it all the way down.

"Are you okay?"

I said that I was. "Things got a little weird there for a minute."

"Porter just wants you to like him, that's all."

"I know. He's okay."

"Why don't you come along, then? We both want you to."

"I would, honest, but I want to call Rachel. I saw her before and . . ."

"Everything's okay?" she said hopefully.

"A lot better."

She leaned into the car then and kissed me twice.

Once on each cheek, like a French hero. "You go on. I'll see you at home."

I eased the car onto the narrow blacktop. Above me the neon dress blinked and fell away. Behind me stood my mom. She was wearing see-through shoes, and a robe with a dragon on it, and I loved her. Ahead of me Rachel waited. I loved her, too, and she might have to move tomorrow or next month or never.

Nothing was like I had ever imagined it would be, but — can you believe it? — I'd never been happier in my life.